FLEXIN ON MY EX WITH A BOSS 3

THE FINALE

JENICA JOHNSON

SHAN PRESENTS, LLC

Flexin' on My Ex with A Boss 3

Copyright by @ Jenica Johnson

Published By: Shan Presents

www.shanpresents.com

SUBSCRIBE

Text Shan to 22828 to stay up to date with new releases, sneak peeks, contest, and more...

WANT TO BE A PART OF SHAN PRESENTS?

To submit your manuscript to Shan Presents, please send the first three chapters and synopsis to submissions@shanpresents.com

PREVIOUSLY IN PART 2...

Bash

I finally felt like Yahria and I were on the same frequency. She was glowing from her pregnancy and today was our reveal party to find out what we were having. Yahria dried off and oiled her small protruding stomach. She wasn't very big, but I didn't expect her to be with her small structure. The way she focused on her stomach and thighs with the stretch mark cream was hilarious.

"If you get stretch marks, you still gon' be fine Yahria."

"This is my body and I don't want no damn tiger stripes. I like wearing my crop tops and shit and I don't want to look like them girls on Facebook with them damn things hanging out."

"Body appreciation, baby. If you get them, just think 'bout why they are there. You brought life into this world. Look at them as superwoman wounds or something. A part of me hopes you get some so you can get over being so self-conscious 'bout it."

"Don't wish that on me. I'm not self-conscious. I just don't want them, is that okay?"

"Whatever makes you feel good 'bout yourself. All that red ass hair can fall out right now, and I'll still be here making love to your ass. Your beauty

ain't on the outside, Yahria. Your outer appearance will never be the same, but the inside tells who you are. I love you no matter what changes on the outside. Besides, after this one, we got 'bout three more to have."

"Help me gawd. Let me see how I'm going to be with this one first."

I grabbed her around her waist and pulled her in between my legs. The pregnancy had her nipples two shades darker and it was the sexiest thing to me. Caressing her body, I made sure to touch all her favorite spots before my hands found their way between her legs. The way Yahria's body responded to my touch had me so hard it was hurting. I raised her on the bed as I got on the floor and rested my head on the bed so she could sit it on my face. She was mine and I had no problem showing her how much I enjoyed tasting her.

As all her nectar dripped down my chin, I eased her down on my dick. She slowly rotated her hips as we stared into each other's eyes. My heart skipped a beat just thinking about what would happen if I lost her. She made me so much better when I was depressed and was afraid to say it. She broke me down to the point I had to be patient in loving her. The way she commanded me to respect her after she realized she deserved it, turned me on in a major way.

"I love you," I told her.

"I love you too."

That was her first time telling me she loved me. I was always the one to tell her and I never got mad when she didn't say it back because I knew how hard it was to say it. If she stuck this thing out with me, I was going to give her and my children the world. Yahria deserved that and so much more. She stepped in and connected with my son without trying. What more could I ask for at this moment?

The alarm clock went off signifying that our time was up, and it was time to get our day started for real this time. I pulled Yahria into me as we both climaxed until we were dizzy. She knew them slow nuts fucked me up every time. Now I was seeing stars and it was going to take me another ten minutes before I could move from this position.

"You know what the hell you be doing. Get your ass up and get ready," I popped her on her ass.

"You love it," she laughed as she entered the bathroom.

We got dressed and headed to the venue that Neca had set up. I wanted to hire Keysa one last time but Yahria shut all that down and left everything in the hands of Neca. She had good taste so I'm sure it was going to be good. Yahria was nice enough to invite my mama and I was still unsure on how she was going to come in acting. For the sake of everyone, I hoped shit went smooth and my baby could enjoy her day with no glitches.

Neca rented a castle on the most expensive piece of land in the outskirts of the city. She was spending so much money, I had to put a cap on her ass but from the gate all the way to the circular driveway was decorated perfectly. Neither, Yahria or I had a lot of friends, but we were thankful for the people that were there. We entered the castle where a crown was placed on both of our heads and we were walked down the red carpet to our thrones. In between us was a small throne with a baby crown on it.

"This is so cute."

"Yea, Neca did her thing. I figured she would go all out for you though."

Neca was walking towards us with her African attire on. She was taking this hostess shit to the extreme.

"How did I do?" She asked us.

"You showed out girl." Yahria got up and hugged her.

"Y'all don't have to move from up here 'cause I have people here to serve you guys. You know Big Ma threw down on this food so just enjoy each other's company and smile for the pictures. We got positive vibes only today so we not letting nobody steal the joy from finding out if I'm having a niece or not," Neca sassed.

The atmosphere was so right, and I think it had something to do with my mama not being here. Yahria and I took pictures and even though we didn't have to move, we got up and mingled with our guests before the big reveal. I was chopping it up with a few of my boys when my mama pranced her ass through the door. Yahria and Neca were talking so I headed back towards her, so we can do the reveal and get the hell on. I still wasn't fucking with my mama, but this was her grandchild and that was the only reason she was invited.

"Hey, let's get the reveal over with. My mama just got here, and I don't want her ruining shit for you," I told Yahria.

Neca immediately grabbed the microphone to get everyone's attention.

My mama walked towards us, but I gave her a look to let her know not to fuck with me right now. She stopped and stood with the crowd as Neca had us both put our hand on the baby crown.

"You ready?" I asked Yahria.

"Are you ready?"

"I'm going to count to three," Neca said. "One…two…three!"

We lifted the crown and there was a pair of pink diamond earrings. Yahria jumped up and down with Neca. I knew this was going to be my little girl. It was something I wanted. Yahria was crying when she made it to me.

"Are you happy or did you want another little boy?"

"Hell nah! I always wanted a little girl. I'm ready to spoil her little ass."

"I'm so excited to have a lil' me running 'round."

"I need prayer now 'cause if she anything like you, I'm in trouble."

"Congratulations you guys," my mama approached.

"Thank you," Yahria replied.

"Subashtian, can I talk to you in private."

"Nah, you broke that privacy on Thanksgiving. Say what you got to say or do you need a few glasses of wine?"

My mama shifted her eyes to Yahria and back at me. Neca came closer to Yahria just in case something popped off. I stepped in between Yahria and my mama because whatever she was about to say could be the cause of her getting her ass beat today. I've held Yahria back long enough, so I was hoping she was coming to apologize.

"Bash, I have some disturbing news and I would rather tell you in private so I won't ruin her moment."

"Mama, say it now or leave."

"It's about Esha."

"What about her? It's been a year now, I moved on and her parents know this already. So, what's the problem?" I asked.

"She's…she's here," my mama confessed.

"Get the hell outta here. Are you on something?" I laughed until Esha walked into the same room as me.

"I know somebody muthafuckin' lyin'," Neca said behind me. "What the hell kind of games y'all playing?"

My feet were stuck and my heart was beating against my chest like the African drums that were playing through the speakers. This couldn't be true. There was no way in hell the mother of my son was walking towards me. I was trying to gather myself quickly because Neca and Yahria were saying shit amongst each other but I still couldn't move.

"Bash! Bash!" Yahria shook me. "You played me for the last damn time. I can't believe you would play with someone's feelings like this," Yahria cried.

My mouth was moving but nothing was coming out. I looked from her to Esha and back at Yahria. What had just happened to my life?

"Neca, get all my baby shit and take me the fuck home." Yahria stormed off.

"Umm, listen up. This party is over; you know it's a girl. Could everyone leave the building please?" Neca said over the microphone.

Yahria came back towards us with vengeance in her eyes.

"Bitch, I know you had something to do with this and when I find out, I'm gon' beat your muthafuckin' ass," she told my mama.

When she smirked at Yahria during this difficult time, Yahria punched my mama so hard in her face blood started pouring from her lips. It was like she blacked out after that and started beating the hell out of my mama.

"Nobody better touch her either. Let your mama take this ass whooping. She been trying my baby long enough," Big Ma threatened.

"She's pregnant," I told her.

"If she lose it, it's your bitch ass mama fault," she told me. "Neca, grab Yah-Yah and let's get the hell out of here before I shoot this shit up."

I had my mama lying on the floor bleeding, Esha standing there like a lost child, and the love of my life walking out the door carrying a piece of me with her. Esha reached out and touched my arm and that fire and spark I used to feel was no longer there. She didn't even look the same. It was some funny shit going on and I needed answers and the person with them all was lying on the floor fighting for her life.

1

Yah-Yah

"I KNEW that bitch ass nigga wasn't shit!" I screamed as I snatched all my shit off the hangers. "He did all that lying 'bout he'll never hurt me and shit."

I was clearing as much of my shit out as I could because I wasn't coming back. My head was hurting so bad and I'm sure my blood pressure was through the roof. Dragging my shit through the closet, I kicked a few bags down the stairs for Neca to grab and load in the car. When Bash made it home, I wouldn't be there. Him, his mama, and his bitch could have this shit. It wasn't worth the stress. The dick was damn good but not worth my sanity.

"Yah-Yah, come on, leave the rest of that shit. I know that bitch called the police on you," Big Ma stated standing in the door.

I descended the steps with tears rolling down my face and a pain that had my heart in a chokehold. There was no way to be tough about this situation. My heart was aching so bad that it was knocking the breath out of my body. Big Ma saw the hurt in my eyes so she met me at the last step and wrapped her arms around me. That only made me cry worse, I broke down right there in her arms. The pain was unbearable.

"Come on y'all," Neca said.

"Let me get my car keys."

"Girl, you can't drive in your condition," Neca said.

"I'm not leaving my car here. That's my damn car, and I'm taking it. Just drive behind me."

Pulling out of the driveway, I looked in the rearview mirror at the house that I occupied with Bash. Everything we had was fake and I felt played. My daughter moving around in my stomach reminded me that Bash would be a pain in my ass for the next eighteen years.

I ended right back where I started, only this time, I had my own account with money in it and I had a successful business so I would be in my own place in no time. Neca unloaded her car, while I made room for the stuff in the house. Big Ma was fussing because I wouldn't sit down and rest but my adrenaline was still racing and, while I had the energy, I wanted to get all my stuff in the house.

"I think that's all of it. But let's talk 'bout how you beat the hell outta that boy mama," Neca said, laughing.

"I wanted to kill her ass. Inviting her was a big mistake, and I should've listened to my intuition. That bitch did exactly what she said she was gon' do too. She ruined my shit intentionally. Can y'all believe Bash stood there and let all of it go down like a bitch? I'm so disappointed in him that I could spit in his fucking face."

"Speaking of Bash, here he go calling." Neca handed me my phone.

I ignored the call and sat down on the sofa. I missed him already but everyone knew the love he had for Esha. He made that clear to me the day we started kicking it. The way he looked at her when she walked her ass in my shit. I could feel it and I wasn't about to stand in their way.

"I'm 'bout to go shower and lay down before I end up at the hospital. I really thank y'all for being there for me."

"Guh, please! You my best friend. You know I'll go all the way to the end with you," Neca told me. "Love you, girl, and call me if you need me. I don't care if it's to go beat Bash's ass."

We shared a laugh and hug before Neca left. I got up to walk to my room when my phone started ringing again.

"Big Ma, just turn it off. I can't deal with nothing else tonight. I'll deal with it tomorrow or maybe I won't deal with it at all."

"It's whatever you want me to do, baby, I got you. Go lay down."

I grabbed a few things to take a quick shower before getting in my bed. My knuckles were swollen, I had scratches on my face and a small cut on my knee. Things happened so fast, I'm not sure how half those things happened. All I wanted was to be happy and birth a healthy baby without any complications. Bash was worried about me dying during childbirth so I tried my best to rest to ease his mind. Kelly got what she deserved tonight, but I still felt like it wasn't enough.

Sleep didn't come easy for me tonight. It was now close to three in the morning and I was still up looking at the window, rubbing my stomach. It was like my daughter knew her daddy wasn't laying next to me. Bash went to sleep every night talking to her and rubbing her to sleep. Tonight, she was doing flips and making my stomach hurt. No matter what I said to her and how much I rubbed, she was not going to sleep anytime soon.

My head was hurting so bad the next morning that I had no choice but to go to the doctor who then sent me straight to the hospital. My blood pressure was extremely high and she was afraid that I may be at stroke level. I didn't tell Big Ma or nobody where I was going. If I was going to relax, I needed to just stay up here by myself for a few days.

"You really need to relax while you're here. I don't know what has your blood pressure so high but I need you to let it go," my night nurse stated.

"It's a broken heart, but I'm letting go."

"For the sake of your baby, it's a must you take care of yourself."

She finished up and turned my lights out. The only thing on was the television. I was sitting here watching some dumb ass show about a girl marrying a nigga and he had a whole bitch in another state. It was like looking at myself but her ass stayed even after her husband told her he wanted both of them.

"She better than me, I ain't sharing no dick," I said out loud.

Because I didn't rest last night, I was able to fall asleep easily.

~

THREE DAYS LATER, I was released to go home. My blood pressure was down but my heart was still aching. I intentionally left my phone off in my purse so I could focus on getting better for my daughter. When I powered it back on, messages and voicemails were popping up back to back. Majority of them were from Bash but fuck him and his mammy too. Big Ma called and left me two nasty voicemails so she was the first one I called.

"I'm on the way home, Big Ma."

"Where the fuck you been the last seventy-two hours? The police got a warrant for your arrest, Bash brought his fine ass by here and slept on the sofa, and Neca 'round here losing her mind."

"I was in the hospital but back up, a warrant for my arrest? For what?"

"That bitch pressed charges on you. Her ass laid up in the hospital with a broken collarbone, fractured wrist, and a few stitches in the back of her head. I wish the hoe would've died."

"Shit, me too. I'll come home and take a shower so I can turn myself in."

"No hell! We 'bout to go on the run like Madea did. Hell you mean turn yourself in?"

"Man I'm not 'bout to be running Big Ma. I'll go do the damn time 'cause I'm tired at this point."

"Well, Bash just left and I don't know if he coming back."

"Why the hell you let him in?"

"Shit, I don't know. His eyes were red and he looked sick as hell. He hadn't slept since the reveal party and you not talking to him."

"Fuck him!! I'm on the way and while I'm there, if he comes, don't let him in."

Bash could be sick and crying all he wanted to, the shit wasn't going to change my mind about how I felt right now. I pulled up to the house as the cops pulled back up.

"Yahria Moss?" The officer tapped on my window.

"Yes?"

"Step out of the car please."

I slipped my phone in my purse and got out of the car.

"You are under arrest for aggravated assault with a deadly weapon."

"Wait...I ain't have no damn weapon."

He ignored me and finished reading me my rights. Big Ma came running out the door as he was placing me in the back seat.

"Big Ma, just get my purse and lock my car up. I'll call you when I can."

Sitting in the cramped-up backseat with my big stomach and handcuffs tightly grasping my wrist, sent my blood pressure back up. If something happened to my daughter during this ordeal, they might as well throw the key away because I was going after everybody ass that was involved in this bullshit.

"Turn to the left," the woman taking my mugshot told me. "Now turn forward."

I did what she told me making sure I had a mug the whole time. If I could have shot a bird, I would have. Nobody knew it but my heart was cold as fuck now and anybody coming behind Bash was going to go through pure hell. Whatever the judge threw at me, I was gone take that shit and roll with it. In the back of my mind, I wish the bitch would have died.

2

Bash

STANDING in my mirror with a towel wrapped around my waist, I ran my fingers through my hair and down my face. It's been four fucking days since I talked to Yahria. Ninety-six damn hours of her not returning my calls and texts. I went and slept on the sofa at Big Ma house thinking her ass was coming home but she never did. I didn't do good with stress and I was on the verge of fucking snapping.

I slipped on some clothes and headed downstairs to laughter and food being cooked, but wasn't shit funny to be laughing at. Without even heading that way, I grabbed my keys and attempted to walk out the door but was stopped by the devil herself.

"Son, Esha is cooking breakfast for you and E'shon. Come sit down and eat with your family."

I clenched my jaws to stop from snapping on her. She got released from the hospital and came straight here like she lived here.

"She ain't my muthafucka family. Bitch been gon' a year and pop up at me and my girl shit and you think I'm 'bout to sit down with her? Shit, my son don't even want to be 'round her ass. I wish y'all would get the fuck out so I can bring my baby back home."

"She'll never take you back now that she knows Esha is home. Just get over the shit and start working on getting your family in order."

"Get the fuck outta my house before I get back. If I find out you had anything to do with this, I promise you I'll kill you myself," I kissed her forehead and left.

It was mean what I said to her but I meant every word. I would kill my mama if she purposely sabotaged my relationship with Yahria and I wasn't going to feel shit when it happened. Now that Yahria was gone, I was thinking about all that shit she used to tell me about my mama and I never believed it. All our conversations played in my head as I headed back to Big Ma's again. The person I needed answers from was Esha but I was too fucking mad to talk to her ass. She tried all night after the reveal party to talk to me until I snapped on her ass and she hadn't said anything else to me.

Big Ma was sitting on the porch with her phone to her ear when I pulled up. She didn't get off the phone until I reached the porch. From what I could hear on my way up to the porch, Yahria had been picked up by the police and she was trying to figure out if she had a bond.

"You said the police came and picked her up?" I asked without speaking.

"Yea, your bitch ass mama pressed charges against my baby. She got a lot of mouth but can't take an ass whooping."

"How long ago that been?" I asked.

"It's been 'bout three hours and they not telling me shit. Neca ready to go get her but they say they don't have any information."

"I'll be back," I told her.

Everybody in my family was about to get on my damn bad side. Yahria was pregnant with my child and I knew damn well it was my auntie fault that my mama pressed charges and they weren't giving her a bond. My auntie knew not to fuck with me like this. It was

Wednesday and one of her late days at her office. When I entered her office, her secretary knew by the look on my face not to fuck with me.

"Why did I know you were going to show your ass up," my auntie Dawn said without looking up.

"Why the fuck y'all trying my patience? You out of all people know not to fuck with me, auntie." I paced her floor trying to keep my ears from ringing.

"My hands are tied, Subashtian."

"Bullshit and you gotdam know it." I slammed my fist down on her desk, startling her. "Y'all plotted and planned this shit knowing my baby had a fucking record. I don't give fuck if I got to clear all my accounts she getting out this bitch. If I got to get my lawyer involved, I'll make sure your whole operation goes down so how you want to play this shit?"

"Subashtian, there's no need for you to call that damn grease ball of a lawyer you have."

"Release her then."

"I can't sign off on it because Kelly is my sister so I can't get involved."

"Bitch, find a way to get involved. You want to be a part of everything else, so pick your phone up and make some calls. I'll sit here and wait." I sat and got comfortable on her sofa. "I got all damn day as long as Yahria Moss locked up."

"I can get you escorted out of here you know."

"You may, but you'll never be able to sleep comfortably and you know it. Gon' head and pick the phone and do what you do best even if that means opening your legs to married men."

"Nah, that's your nasty ass mama. I like mine single and young."

"Yea, okay. I know more than you think."

She started tapping her keyboard on her laptop with an attitude. She picked up the phone and dialed a number before speaking into the phone.

"Hey, has innate Moss been before the judge?"

I couldn't hear what was said but she glanced at me quickly before clearly her throat.

"I understand all of that. Bring her to me in about twenty minutes." She said before hanging up.

"You a lying ass muthafucka. I knew you were holding her in there. Make sure you remember these games you playing."

"It was not my fault. Usually, you don't see the judge right away but I'm making an exception. Now you can wait outside and I'll call you when she comes down."

I didn't move because I told her I wasn't going anywhere and I meant it.

"Subashtian, the best I'm going to be able to do for her is a bond and a court appearance with your mama but I will not be the judge on Yahria's case. You know your mama don't fight fair. That's why y'all in this shit now."

"What does that mean?"

"Nothing...nothing! Just make sure she stays away from your mama until they've been to court."

"Don't worry 'bout that. They will never cross paths again."

"Make sure of it."

"You got my word, auntie, damn."

"I'm just saying, it seems you having a hard time keeping the women in your life under control. I thought you could at least do that."

"Don't poke the damn bear. Time is ticking."

"I need privacy so when I talk with her she won't flip out when she sees you and I have to throw her back in jail."

"She not gon' flip."

"Ha! Yahria, is going to slap the shit out of you for this bullshit y'all pulled."

"I didn't do a damn thing. I was blindsided too."

"And what did you do about it?"

She was right. I hadn't even handled the situation because I was so busy chasing Yahria to make sure she was okay.

"That's what I thought. I bet your mama at your house now running it like it's hers. You weak for your mama and that's under-standable but it's time to open your eyes and see what's really going on. Now get out my damn office so I can get this girl home with her pregnant ass."

"Listen, I know my mama is your sister and all but you should always want to do what's right."

"And so should you," she said before shooing me off.

I waited outside the courthouse on Yahria to walk out. I was nervous about seeing her because she was going to flip when she saw me. It's been four days since Esha popped up on us and I had no idea what was going through Yahria's head. However she acted, I was willing to take that shit as long as she didn't leave me and my son. We needed her like it was the air that we breathed. E'shon wasn't fucking with Esha and if it wasn't for my mama, he wouldn't even be around her.

Almost two hours later, Yahria emerged from the building with a scold on her face. Her stomach was huge and I watched as she rubbed her stomach before looking in my direction and walking towards me. From the look on her face, she was with the shits but I was ready. I stepped out of the car as she stepped down from the curb. She didn't say one word to me. Yahria just stood there staring up at me. All the hurt was evident in her eyes. Out of nowhere, she slapped me so hard one of my nose rings fell out.

"Take me the fuck home and don't you ever in your fuckin' life say shit else to me," she said getting in the car and slamming the door.

I looked on the ground for my nose ring but couldn't find it. My nose was bleeding but I couldn't get in the car with her right now so I made her wait until I calmed down and hoped that she was calming down too so we could at least talk like adults. When I got in the car, she was looking out of the window. I was glad that she didn't have her phone because I know she would've called Neca to come get her instead of riding with me.

"Baby," I started before she put her hand up to stop me from talking.

"Bash, don't say shit to me before I'm tempted to beat your ass. Take me home and leave me the fuck alone."

"You not gon' hear me out."

"'Bout what? What can you say when the love of your life pops her dead ass back up in your life? Take me home Bash," she said holding back her tears.

My heart was breaking hearing her voice cracking. As far as I knew, I had never broken a girl's heart. My father taught me how to treat women, especially a woman you love. You don't intentionally hurt them. I had no idea what was going on and I wasn't worried about it at the moment. All I wanted to know was, was Yahria going to stick with me or not.

I drove to Big Ma house in silence. The radio played in the background and my phone went off a few times but other than that everything was silent. I stole a few glances at Yahria and her stomach when I got chance but she was still looking out the window like she was annoyed that she was even around me. Yahria thought she was going to just hop out of my car without talking to me but that shit wasn't about to happen. She had her hand on the door as soon as I turned the corner to her house.

"Yahria, wait. Can we talk?" I grabbed her other arm lightly.

"I'm trying to count to ten in my head so I won't knock your damn head off. Get your damn hands off of me. You probably been laid up with your baby mama and shit."

"I ain't touched or talked to that girl since all this shit went down."

Yahria gave me a look like she knew I was lying. I hated Pharaoh for what he did to her because now I was fighting to keep her heart and she wasn't listening to shit I had to say. She climbed out of the car but not without me climbing out too. I left the car running with the keys in it and everything just to talk to her.

"Yahria!" I called out to her. "Yahria, please stop walking away." She kept walking until she made it to the porch. She was standing on the top step as I stood at the bottom. The tears that were coming from her eyes let me know the pain she was feeling. Hell, I was feeling it too.

"Bash, me and you are over, okay. Please just let me deal with this shit on my own. I'm cool with just being your baby mama. I'm not gon' bother you and blow your phone up at night or none of that shit.

I'm leaving it in your hands if you want to be in your daughter's life or not."

"Yahria, why you talking like you ain't where I want to be at? I don't want you to be my baby mama, I want you as my wife."

"Bash, please just stop," she sniffled. "Just a few months ago, you were depressed because you lost the love of your life. She's back now so you can go be a family like you always wanted to be. This shit we had was never real; I was just something to keep your mind off of her. I'm trying my best to deal with shit without stressing my child out."

"Baby, I don't want you stressed out. I don't want her, I want you. Why else am I here? You making this shit seem like I knew what was going on."

"Is she at your house?" Yahria asked with tears still running down her face.

"Yea, but..."

"Bash, there are no buts. Go home and be with your family. Tell your mama she won and whatever beef we had is over. I just don't want to go and do no jail time and I'm 'bout to have my baby. She won," Yahria broke down crying.

I walked up the four steps to try to wrap her in my arms and was shocked when she let me. This shit was hurting me more than I expected. Seeing her cry was the hardest thing in the world to do.

"How could you do this to me?" She slapped me twice.

"I didn't do anything, baby."

"You promised me, Bash. You promised me that you would never break my fuckin' heart. You broke all your promises and now you standing here telling me that bitch at your house? I fuckin' hate your ass."

"I told them to leave but I've been trying to chase you so we could talk. Fuck that hoe! I'm here with you and my daughter. Does that count for something?"

"No! When you leave me, you going right back over there to be with them."

"Shit! You want me to FaceTime you when I put them out? I don't give a fuck 'bout nobody but you and my kids."

"Why did you choose me?"

"What?"

"Why me? All those *I love you's* don't mean shit to my broken heart right now, Bash. Just go get your shit together with your family. You don't owe me shit."

"I'm not leaving," I told her.

"Bash, for real, leave. I don't want you no more."

"Baby, you not serious right now. You upset."

"Bitch, you haven't seen upset. Get the fuck away from me before you have more than a few welts on your face. When I'm ready to talk to you, I'll call you."

She wiped her face before Big Ma opened the screen door where she was standing the whole time to make sure shit didn't get out of hand. I heard Yahria breakdown as soon as Big Ma closed the door. I walked back to my car and sat there with my head in my hands trying to gather myself before I headed home.

E'shon ran up to me when I opened the door but I didn't have the energy to even be bothered with him. I walked past him and headed for the steps to go to my room.

"Did I just see you walk pass your son? You mean to tell me this bitch got you so lovesick that you ignoring your son?" My mama nagged.

"Mama leave me the fuck alone right now."

"Excuse me?"

"I said, leave me the fuck alone. I thought I told y'all to be the fuck outta my house?"

"Don't you ever in your life talk to me like that. I let you do that shit because that lil' bitch of yours had you acting funny towards me. Your family is back together and you need to act accordingly."

"Family? Only family in this bitch is my son! Fuck you and that coke head ass bitch you brought back in my life."

"Subashtian, you don't mean that. You love Esha and you need to make this work for your son."

"Stay out my business. It's your fault all this shit going on. I see your lil' damn games but guess what. I don't want Esha so take her ass back where the fuck she was. Where her ass at anyway?"

"She's upstairs in the bedroom. She was tired so I let her go rest."

"Go rest where?" I asked my mama.

"She's back in the bedroom she supposed to be in."

I took the steps two at a time to my bedroom to see Esha laid in my bed.

"Get the fuck up right now."

"Bash, what...what did I do?" Esha asked nervously.

I slammed the door to my bedroom and stepped in Esha face. My heart was beating against my chest so hard, I could hear it in my ears.

"Where the fuck you been at? And if you lie to me, I'll break your fuckin' neck in here," I warned.

Esha swallowed real hard before she looked to the ground and back up into my eyes. The same eyes that I found so much love in, betrayed me for a whole year.

"I didn't want you to know I had started back getting high my last few months with our son. I asked your mom to help me get clean. I wanted real help so I went across seas and got the best treatment possible. I'm so sorry," she let her tears fall.

I gripped her around her neck and slammed her head against the headboard.

"You mean to tell me, you got high while my son was inside of you? You couldn't wait nine fuckin' months before you started shootin' up? I should kill your dirty ass right now but my son is right outside the door and he don't know your trifling ass yet."

I released her neck, leaving my massive hand print on her neck. She let her tears fall but I wasn't moved.

"Get the fuck outta of my room. Don't bring your ass 'round me until I figure out what the fuck to do with you. If I'm in the kitchen, you better move the fuck outa my way. Bond with your son and don't worry 'bout me wanting your ass back."

Esha scurried out of the bed and I noticed she squeezed her ass in a pair of Yahria tights and shirt.

"Take that shit off you got on. You got some damn nerve putting my girl shit on," I scolded.

"I don't have anything else to put on," she whined.

"My mama been helping you so go tell her to buy you some shit."

Esha slowly stepped out of the clothes, displaying her body. Esha body was banging still and I was quickly reminded of all the sex we used to have right here in this room. My mind was thinking but my dick wasn't moving. The tattoo of my initials right above her pussy did send a little bit of blood flow to my dick but not enough for her to get a rise out of me. I went in the bathroom and threw her a towel to wrap around her. As soon as I opened the door to my bedroom, Yahria was standing there with death in her eyes. It was the same look she had at the reveal party when she damn near killed my mama.

"Baby, it ain't what you thinking," I tried to explain before she started swinging.

For Yahria to be so small, she packed a punch like a nigga from the streets. I was ducking and dodging her blows as Esha ran her naked scary ass out the bedroom instead of explaining what the hell happened in here.

"Yahria...stop," I begged her after each blow.

"You a bitch ass nigga. You didn't expect for me to pop up did you?"

I was finally able to grab her hands and push her on the bed. Her stomach was stopping me from sitting on her ass because she was trying to kick a nigga in the nuts.

"Calm the fuck down before you hurt yourself and my baby," I told her.

"Get the fuck up off of me. Why the fuck she in here naked?"

"Are you gon' calm down?"

"Yea," she said out of breath.

She had my lip swelling up and I could taste the blood inside my mouth.

"I'm gon' let you up but don't put your hands on me again, Yahria. You been beating my ass all day for no reason. That's your last time."

"Just get off of me Bash," she tried to push me off but I wouldn't budge.

Slowly, I raised up off of Yahria as the tears ran down the side of her face. If I wasn't afraid that she would slap the shit out of me, I would kiss all of them away but she was on ten right now and I didn't know what was going through her mind. She struggled to get up so I reached out to help her.

"Move your damn hand," she slapped my hand away. "I don't know where your damn hands been. You got this bitch all in here naked and shit with your dick hard."

"What you saw is not what you thinking happened in here."

"You couldn't wait to get me out of here to sleep with her."

"I didn't fuckin' sleep with her. What the hell you want me to do to prove to you I want you. I don't give a damn 'bout her."

"You don't have to prove shit. I'm just coming to get a few things I left so I won't have any other excuse to come over here."

Yahria entered our closet and I followed her trying to explain myself until my mama brought her dumb ass in there. Now, I promised my auntie that I was going to keep them apart but in my eyes, this was Yahria's house and my mama was a visitor.

"What the hell she doing here?" My mama asked.

"Ma, go on now. You all in here minding my damn business," I told her.

"You better tell that bitch to get the fuck outta of my face before I kill her ass this time," Yahria spazzed.

"Who, bitch?" My mama taunted.

"Bitch, I'm talking to your bitter ass. You think you standing there with them cast and shit on, this time, I'm gon' finish the job and go do my time. Get your ass outta my face and go tend to your daughter in law."

"She'll always be better than your dumb ass. My son never loved you. You were a charity case and an easy fuck. Bash get this trash out of here," my mama stated.

I watched her walk out of my closet and heard the door close when I turned around to see Yahria standing there with tears streaming down her face.

"That's all I was to you?" she asked, on the verge of breaking down.

"Man, hell nah! I never looked at you like a charity case and definitely not an easy fuck. I don't have unprotected sex with women that are easy. You carrying my child, you have to know you mean something to me."

"I should've never came over here. To see the man, I love, in here with his first love and she's naked, really did something to me. I should not have overreacted 'cause really y'all relationship wasn't over. I'm sorry for putting my hands on you. I'll make sure to let you know what's going on with the baby. This shit is just too stressful for me to deal with and I can't fight anymore over a nigga. I'm tired and my daughter's life is way more important than this shit we got going on."

I grabbed her and kissed her lips so she could stop talking like we weren't going to be together. There was no way I was going to let her walk out of my life after she made it better. True enough, I had some shit to clarify with Esha but there was no me and her after what she just told me. My future was with Yahria and my kids.

"Bash," Yahria said between kisses. "Please, stop."

I stopped kissing her but not before wiping her tears away.

"I love you, Yahria and I wish you would just let me fix this."

"I love you too, Bash but I got to get away from and this toxic relationship. As long as your mother is in your ear there will never be a me and you."

Yahria picked up her small bag and walked out of the closet. My head was spinning watching her walk out yet again. Every time she told me she didn't want me, my heart skipped a beat. I wasn't giving up though.

3

Y ahria

ESHA'S naked ass body was the only vision I saw as I laid in the hotel room. As much as I wanted to slap the shit out of her, a part of me felt like she was Kelly's lapdog and there was no real beef with her. Shit, we both loved the same man. Why was I going to hate her? I wasn't a jealous bitch by far. Everyone knew I was a petite female. Most wondered why men wanted me because women like Kesh and Esha were killing it with their bodies. Bash was completely dressed when Esha walked out but his dick print was showing which is what set me off. He was still a man and the men I knew would stick their dick in anything.

I hadn't eaten anything since I left Bash's house yesterday. All I could do was lay in bed and stare out of the window that over looked downtown. My phone was on do not disturb because I didn't want to be bothered. The world had ended for me when this bitch stepped back in the picture. She wasn't my concern though. If Bash wanted me, he had a lot of stuff to do to get me back. My feelings were gone and I didn't care what happened between us. My bank account was sitting pretty decent and I wasn't in the need to beg anyone.

"Room service," a woman busted in the room.

"I don't need anything," I said, pulling the cover over my head so she wouldn't see me.

"You sure? No towels, wash clothes or anything?"

"I said I didn't need anything," I told her.

"Okay, well call downstairs if you need anything."

I didn't even turn around to see if she was gone. My focus was staring at the skyline until she spoke again.

"Wait a minute. Are you Yahria? My best friend got a dress made by you for her baby shower. You are the shit. What are you doing here?"

She sounded like she was a damn fan. I wasn't nobody, at least that's what I felt like.

"I'm trying to get my mind together before I head back home."

"Well, while you're here please let me know if you need anything. There are some good spots around here to eat and hang out."

"I won't be doing neither but thank you."

"If you change your mind, I put my number next to your phone."

I waved her off and laid there with tears feeling my eyes. My life was going so good and it was pulled right from under me. I should've never fucked with Bash in the first place. He was way out of my league when we first started talking. It was a challenge for me and him. The balance that we gave each other was out of this world. My room phone started ringing but I ignored. It started again so I answered.

"Guh come open up this damn door. You got folks calling your cell phone and shit and you laid up over here in another city."

"Neca, how did you know where I was?"

"One of the damn workers posted your car on damn Instagram. I was scrolling through the random pictures and there was your car. Now, get your ass up or I'm using the key that I paid the desk dude for."

"I swear I can't have no privacy."

"Ain't no damn privacy in this friendship when you going through."

I hung up the phone and opened the door to Neca standing there dripping in designer clothes and that damn chain that Bash made.

"So, you drive your ass a whole hour away just to get a room?" Neca asked, placing her purse down on the sofa.

"If I would've known my car got me attention, I would've went and got a rental."

"You the only one with that car so of course it's going to catch attention. Then you got the nerve to be riding 'round with a tag that says *Bash GRL* on it."

"I got to change that immediately."

"Please, tell me you've been washing your ass."

"Yes, Neca. I'm not that damn heart-broken."

"Well, put something on and let's go hang out. I know you 'bout to bust but getting you out would do you some good."

"I don't feel like it. I just want to lay here and cry and think 'bout how my life could have been."

"Nah, we ain't doing no weak shit like that. Get up and put some clothes on. Fix your face and let me do something to this hair. The only way to get over a nigga is fix yourself up and make him miss what he had."

"I hear you."

"Listen, you can't make a nigga act right, but you can make them wish they did."

I got my ass back out the bed and got myself together which took me longer because of my massive stomach and my constant urination. By the time I was finished, I was feeling better and looking better. Neca fixed my hair up nice and my dress looked nice even with my stomach.

After going to dinner we ended up at a nice lounge that was for the grown and sexy. I never knew this small town had so many spots to hang out at. The music felt good to me and even though I couldn't drink I was still enjoying myself. It felt good to just take my mind off of Bash for a little while.

"Ahh, shit!"

"What?" I asked Neca.

"Pharaoh and Gip walking they ass over here."

I sipped on my Shirley Temple and watched the dance floor when Pharaoh's cologne filled my nose. If I ignored him, maybe he would just disappear like he always does. No matter how mad I was with Bash, Pharaoh just couldn't get any of my time. We had our closure and there was nothing else for us to say.

"You gon' act like you don't see me standing here?" Pharaoh asked.

"I'm not obligated to speak to you."

"It would be nice though. It's not like we weren't just together."

"You're right. Hey, Pharaoh," I dryly said.

"Can I get a hug."

"Don't push it too damn far. Hey is good enough for us."

While I was talking to Pharaoh, I paid attention to Neca and Gip. They always had a chemistry that they both tried to ignore. I thought it was cute but Neca said he didn't have enough money. She was shocking me by entertaining him.

"Pregnancy looks good on you. What you doing out here? I'm sure Neca dragged you out of that mansion. Your nigga have a tight grip on your ass."

"Something like that."

"What you having?"

"A girl."

"I bet she's going to be as beautiful as you. I'll make sure to buy a gift and send it through Neca."

"You know she don't fuck with you like that so don't worry 'bout no gift."

"Me and Neca working on our relationship. It ain't easy and I get why she stayed mad with me. You got a real friend there and she riding with you until the wheels fall off. Now that we are no longer together, Neca and I are able to have a decent conversation. She helped me realize how much of a dog I was to you."

"Well, that's good to know. You was a dog but I ain't here to judge you."

"Shit, it's just good you sitting here talking to a nigga. I miss us kicking it."

"I'm sitting here talking to you 'cause I don't have much of a choice and my best friend hugged up with your best friend. Don't get it twisted, though, I'm not giving you too much of my time."

"Still got that smart ass mouth."

"That's never going anywhere."

Pharaoh was looking good or maybe it was because I was in my feelings and wanted to hurt Bash like he hurt me. Pharaoh changed up the way he dressed and carried himself and it made him look a lot more mature than he usually did.

"How are your daughters?" I asked him.

"They doing good. I would love for you meet them one day. My oldest one ask 'bout you all the time."

"Why is that?" I looked at him confused.

"She's eleven and she used to hear me and her mama argue 'bout you all the time. She's curious to know who you are 'cause she think we are still together."

"You need to let her know that we are not together 'cause you couldn't be truthful. No need in letting her think something that's not true. This should be a wakeup call for you. You have two daughters and I know you don't want nobody mistreating them so make sure the next woman you get with, you treat her right."

"I don't want another woman if it ain't you," Pharaoh said, closing the gap between us.

"Pharaoh, please move out of my space. I'm pregnant and I'm not responsible for my actions."

"All I'm asking for is another chance. I'll help you raise your daughter. I know you ain't with that nigga no more; I was just waiting on you to say something."

"How the hell you know my business?"

"I'm in the streets. I know everything."

"I don't need no help raising my child and no I don't want to give you another chance. I'm all out of love for niggas. All of y'all just alike so I'm good."

"Can we at least be friends again? I won't pressure you or anything. I really miss you. Since our friends kicking it, we will see a lot of each other."

"I don't hang out like I used to so I doubt you'll see much of me. There is no hate in my heart for you but I can't kick it with you. I spent the last seven years with you and if I'm 'round you, then feelings may get involved and I don't want you to think there will ever be another us."

"Damn, you can't even let a nigga down lightly."

"I'm at the point in my life where I can't afford to beat 'round the bush no more."

We ended up talking for a few more minutes before I excused myself to go to the bathroom. I needed to breathe because Pharaoh wasn't letting up and it was becoming aggravating. If Neca wasn't ready to leave in the next hour, I was leaving without her. My back was killing me and I was ready to get back in the bed. My ringing phone in my purse made me cut my piss short. Once I saw it was Bash calling, I hit the ignore button and finished up in the bathroom. A text came through from him as I was washing my hands.

Bash: Could you answer the damn phone? I'm trying to make sure you straight. Big Ma said she ain't heard from you and I'm worried.

Me: I'm good!

Bash: Can you meet me. I want to see you.

Me: Nah! We wouldn't be meeting if we were still together. Get off the phone with me and tend to your family.

I put my phone on vibrate and exited the bathroom. Pharaoh was no longer at the table which was perfect for me. As I walked back to the where we were he popped back up. Instead of going back, I exited the club and walked about two blocks and then got an Uber back to the room. I still had two nights left in this room and I was going to make the best out of them. When I got back to the hotel, I jumped in my car and went and loaded up on snacks. The next forty-eight hours was going to consist of junk food and movies on my MacBook.

~

A WEEK LATER...

I agreed for Bash to meet me at the doctor's office just so he could be up to speed on how the baby was doing. The whole time while I laid on the table, he caressed my stomach as our daughter did flips. Occasionally, he would try to touch me in other areas until I slapped his hand away.

"Yahria, looks like you are right on track. You're healthy and the baby is healthy. I am concerned though about the delivery of your baby. You are very small and your daughter appears to be almost seven pounds now. You still have a few weeks to go before she's born but the last few weeks is when the baby gains all their weight. I want you to be prepared to have a Cesarean if necessary."

"I thought we agreed to have a home birth?" Bashed inquired.

"We did but that was before I had to move back with Big Ma. I found a spot but it's not big enough for them to bring that big ass pool and shit in there," I told him.

"You can come back home and we can do it there."

"I'm never coming back home Bash. That is not my home."

"Well dammit find a bigger spot and I'll pay for it."

The midwife cleared her throat because we had totally forgot about her being in the room.

"I'm sorry. I'm still looking forward to the home birth but I'll prepare myself for a cesarean as well."

"Okay, well if there are no questions for me, I'll see you next week."

She washed her hands and exited the room leaving me and Bash in there. He helped me get dressed and checked out. I hit the unlock on my car so fast because I really didn't want to talk. He came and served his purpose and there was nothing else to say. He ended up beating me to my car and leaning up against the door so I couldn't get in.

"Are you gon' find a bigger spot?"

"No Bash! I don't want you paying for shit. I'm going to get what I can afford."

"Why, Yahria? Gotdamn, I'm trying here. I'm not even staying at my own damn house. I let them have that shit. The only reason I go over there is to see my son. I've been between Big Ma house and a hotel. If it wasn't for her then I wouldn't eat. I can't take this shit no more. What you want me to do?"

"Do you want me to give you a cookie or something? I'm not asking you to do anything but let me live my life now. All we have is this little girl in my stomach to worry 'bout. There is no me and you, Bash."

His shoulder slumped and his eyes got glassy. Just his look alone was starting to make me feel bad for being so rough with him. His mouth told me he was trying but it just wasn't enough for me. There was no way he wasn't sleeping with Esha and she was right there in the house. I knew how he was with me and his sexual appetite was extremely high.

"I'll leave you alone. Could you just come here so I can hold you for a second?"

Why...why did my body gravitate towards him. As soon as he placed his arms around me and his Bond No. 9 tickled my nostrils, I was done. My head fell into his chest as he rubbed my back and my heart beat got in sync with his. This felt like where I was supposed to be but that was never going happen. His mama would certainly not let us enjoy our life together.

"I love you, Yahria," Bash said resting his head on top of mine.

The tears welled up in my eyes. Bash sounded so sincere every time he told me he loved me. I didn't doubt it but his heart didn't belong to me. It was like I came in and snatched it when he was still in love with someone else.

"Don't tell me that. My heart can't take that right now."

"I mean it. If I have to spend the rest of my life proving it to you and my daughter that it's y'all that I want, then I will."

"How is E'shon?" I asked.

"He's doing okay. I can tell he misses you. I try to let him bond with his mama but he cries so much when she touches him or anything. Can I bring him to see you?"

"Bash, I don't want to see him knowing that he's going back home to his mama."

"He don't have too. Give me the word and I'll go buy you the biggest house possible. Whatever you want, I'll get it."

"You know that shit don't matter to me, that's why I'm not looking for a bigger spot than the one I found."

"How big is this spot you going to? Will I be able to at least come over or are you gon' keep that a secret and meet me to spend time with my daughter?"

"I may. It depends on how my heart feels towards you."

"I had no idea 'bout none of this baby. Do you believe me?"

"I don't know what to believe, Bash. All I know is right now I don't have the man I fell in love with. You sold me these big ass dreams 'bout being together and here we are hugged up outside of the doctor's office like we hiding our relationship. This is why I never wanted to get pregnant anytime soon."

"I haven't left you. You keep pushing me away. I'm the only one trying though. Do you even want me?"

"Bash, I don't want you."

He pushed me out of his arms and glared at me in disbelief that I was so blunt. Shit, I did want him but I didn't want him if he couldn't control the dumb shit his mama did. She fucked it up real bad for us. Bringing Esha back into Bash's life was the topping on the cake.

"You mean that?" He asked me.

"Yea," I said, looking down on the ground.

He placed a kiss on my lips and walked off to his car. I stood there as he got in and pulled off without saying anything else. Climbing in my car, I broke down crying. I put my foot in my damn mouth knowing I didn't mean that shit.

4

B ash

IT'S BEEN a month since I talk to Yahria. It was like my life was slipping away from me every day that she wasn't with me. I was spending so much money staying at a hotel that I just went and got me a condo just so I didn't have to go home. Life was beating my ass so bad that I hadn't opened my shop in weeks. People were calling my phone but I wasn't answering. Yahria was due to have the baby within the next few weeks and I was hoping to hear from her. Big Ma told me that she had moved. Now, Big Ma told me where she was but I wasn't going to pop up on her. There was no need for me to call or go see her until my daughter gets here. She made it clear she didn't want me and I was done begging.

Yahria made it clear that our issue was my mama. To someone like her, it was easy to just block out her mama but for me, this was the woman that gave me life. I did everything I thought I could to keep her away from Yahria. It wasn't enough and that was my fault but I was still willing to make our relationship work. My ringing phone is the only thing that made me move from the spot I was laying in.

"Yea," I spoke into the phone.

"Bash, could you come get E'shon? Your mama ain't here and he been crying for the last two hours. I've fed him, changed him, and gave him his tablet but it's not working."

"Damn, you his mama and you don't know how to soothe your damn son? Shit, Yahria wouldn't have this problem."

"Really Bash? Don't make me feel bad about this."

"Hell, you should feel bad. Yahria helped raise your son while you were somewhere with a needle in your damn arm. Then you calling me talking 'bout you don't know what to do. I'm on the way and don't be in my damn way when I get there," I told her before hanging the phone up.

I took a quick shower, threw some clothes on and headed to get my son. Pulling up, my lawn was a mess and my cars needed to be washed. Esha was already at the door with E'shon crying. As soon as he saw me he stopped crying and started squirming to try to get out of his mama arms. I grabbed E'shon from her arms and kissed him.

"What is wrong with you, boy? You miss me?"

"I need help around here, Bash."

"For what? This what you and my mama wanted, right? I gave y'all the damn house so take care of it."

"I'm talking about with your son."

"I did it a whole year, you can't do it? Let me know now so I can take him back to my spot with me."

"Your spot?"

"Yep! What you thought this was? I told you I didn't want you. You and my mama thought y'all had this shit figured out didn't you? I'll never want your ass back for the simple fact you knew how much I loved you and you picked drugs over what we had. You put my son's life in jeopardy."

"I...I didn't-."

"Don't even open your mouth to lie to me. I'll make sure y'all straight but you better get out and get you a damn job or something. I'll bring him back in a couple of days," I told her before walking off.

Esha stood there the whole time I placed my son in his seat and pulled off. I didn't ask her ass for diapers, clothes or nothing. She didn't even know how to be a mother to her own son so she definitely couldn't be my woman again. I don't care how much love I had for her it was gone and the only reason I felt sorry for her was because of my son. We did build the house together so it was partly hers so I let her have it. If I wanted Yahria back, then I need to start fresh memories with her.

I went to a few stores to grab my son some things for my spot before we headed home. He was getting sleepy and he hadn't eaten so I slid over to Big Ma house in hopes that Yahria would be there too but mainly to see if she cooked. Since me and Yahria weren't together, I wasn't getting the nice home cooked meals unless I went to Big Ma house. A smile spread across my face when I saw Yahria's car. I grabbed E'shon and grabbed a diaper out of the trunk so he could be changed once I got inside.

It was the middle of winter and Big Ma had the door closed so I had to wait for someone to open and let us in. E'shon laid his head on my shoulder so he could go to sleep until the door opened and Yahria stood there with a sports bra and pajama pants on. Her hair was in four ugly plaits but she was still fine as hell. My son almost jumped out of my arms to get to her. She smiled so big as she struggled to grab him.

"You don't need to be picking him up," I told her.

"I got this. Why are you here anyway?" She asked as she kissed E'shon.

"I came to eat; it has nothing to do with you." I tried to remain hard but I desperately wanted to touch her.

"Let that damn boy in here, shit," Big Ma fussed.

Yahria stepped aside and let me in the house. She closed the door and sat down with E'shon on her lap. He was clinging to her so tight like he was afraid she was going to let him go.

"Gon' in the kitchen and fix you and that baby something to eat.

Don't act like you ain't used to being over here now that she's here. Her big ass over here to eat too," Big Ma stated.

"Don't tell him that! I came over here to get some rest 'cause I been hurting and I didn't want to be alone."

"But your big ass came to eat too, didn't you?" Big Ma asked.

"Hell yea I ate," Yahria laughed.

"Alright then," Big Ma said.

"You been hurting? Why you ain't called me and told me?" I asked her.

"I'm good. Big Ma got me."

"Are you pregnant from Big Ma?"

"Nah, 'cause Big Ma strictly-."

"Big Ma, please," Yahria begged. "I didn't want to bother you 'cause we haven't talked in a month and you hadn't showed up to any appointments."

"Now it's my fault? You told me you didn't want me anymore. Why will I keep letting you snatch my heart every time we 'round each other knowing you will never believe shit I got to say?"

"You still could've took your peasy head ass to that doctor," Big Ma added.

"Being 'round you is hard for me. But my bad for not going to the appointments. If you hurting and not telling me, what makes me think you won't go have the baby without letting me know."

"'Cause I ain't a selfish person. It was just a few contractions, could you please go eat or something," Yahria waved me off.

I left them in the living room while I went in the kitchen to fix me and E'shon something to eat. Big Ma had cooked like it was a Sunday. The turkey wings and the gravy was looking so good that I piled three on my plate along with some greens and macaroni and cheese. She made me forget all about my health when I came over here. I put the plate in the microwave and went to go get E'shon so he could eat but he was asleep on Yahria's chest. I went to grab him and wake him up but she knocked my hand away.

"Leave him alone and let him sleep. He tired as hell. When the last time he got a good night's rest? Have y'all been reading his favorite book?"

"I don't know, I left him with his mama. She called me today saying she needed help with him 'cause he wouldn't stop crying."

"What you mean you left him?"

"I got a new spot and let they ass have the house. He needs to bond with his mama so I left him."

"You don't just leave him like that. Especially with a damn stranger."

"I didn't just leave him. I would go check on him every now and then."

Yahria shook her head and focused her attention back on her phone. She was texting somebody but I couldn't see who it was. My stomach was touching my back so I went back to eat. After I finished, no one was in the living room. It was still early so Big Ma was probably gone to play her numbers and Yahria was more than likely in her room sleep. I walked down the hall to her room and looked in to see her and E'shon sleeping peacefully with the box fan blowing in their faces. Pulling my phone, I had to capture this moment for myself.

There wasn't much room in the bed for me, but I was able to squeeze in behind Yahria and wrap my arms around her stomach. My daughter started moving around letting me know she knew my touch. This is how my life was supposed to be. I let too many people get in between what we had and I needed to get it right so I could have my family back but what was I going to do with Esha? She wasn't just going to let me move on with our son. She didn't have an evil bone in her body but one thing I knew was a jealous woman was dangerous.

As soon as I closed my eyes, Yahria's phone started buzzing. She never kept her phone on vibrate, it was always on because she was a social media junky. I ignored it and tried to drift back to sleep until it started again. It stopped but then a text came through. My mind started getting the best of me and I didn't want to be a possessive baby daddy but the only person that calls back to back and send a text is a nigga or a female that's trying to come through. I talked myself into letting the shit go because we weren't together. The third time it went off, I got out the bed and snatched the phone from the dresser and answered it.

"Yea," I rudely answered.

"Who dis?"

"Bitch ass nigga you know who the fuck this is. Don't call my girl no more, nigga."

"You real funny. I know Yah-Yah ain't your girl no more, nigga. You let your mama come and fuck that up. What you thought she wasn't gon' come holla at a nigga when she knows I'm what she used to?"

My eye sight was becoming blurry as I looked at Yahria lay there peacefully like she ain't slept a wink in days. Was she laying up with this nigga while she was pregnant with my child?

"Don't call this phone no more unless you ready to meet your maker early. It's up to you nigga."

"Man, tell Yah-Yah her real nigga called. Oh before I hang up, tell her I dropped all y'all daughter gifts off at her spot downstairs," he said before hanging up.

I squeezed the hell out of Yahria phone until I heard it crack. Feeling that it wasn't enough, I threw that bitch on the floor and stomped causing both of them to wake up.

"What the hell you doing?" She asked, rubbing her eyes.

I didn't answer her. I kept stomping the shit out of her phone until the little screws were rolling all over the floor. She got out of the bed to see what I was doing and spazzed when she noticed it was her phone.

"Bash, what the fuck," she yelled. "Why would you do that?" She pushed me.

Without thinking I grabbed her by her sports bra and pushed her up against her dresser. I made sure her little ass didn't have anything to hit me with.

"You back with your old nigga now?"

"What? Hell, nah!"

"Why he blowing up your shit then? Why the fuck he knows all our business and shit? You want a nigga to treat you bad so you go running your ass back to him," I shook her.

"I ain't told him nothing," she started to cry.

"You don't want me 'cause of my baby mama who I ain't sleep with in forever but you want his bitch ass, huh? I told you early on that I would kill both of y'all. Let me find out you been laying your pregnant ass down with that nigga while carrying my child. I don't give a fuck 'bout nobody, I'm gon' kill your lil' ass. Call me when it's time for my daughter to enter the world," I told her, grabbing E'shon off the bed and walking out.

5

ah-Yah

I CRIED as I picked up the pieces to my phone. No matter how much I told Bash I didn't want to be with him, I did. He had my heart but it was just hard for me to give him another chance. Seems every time I give people a chance they fuck it up. After cleaning my phone up, I put some clothes on and headed to the hood where I knew Pharaoh had his ass at. It was my fault that he was calling and texting. I gave him my number only because I was feeling vulnerable. As soon as I did it, I knew I had made a mistake.

When Pharaoh started texting me earlier today, I told him to leave me alone. He continued on even when Bash popped up; it seemed like it got worse so I put my phone on vibrate to drown it out. I circled the block a few times and didn't see Pharaoh. His car was parked but he wasn't in sight. Then he popped up with Kesh dirty mouth ass. It didn't matter to me; I parked and wobbled my ass right up to him.

"Why the fuck you telling Bash all these damn lies?" I asked, mushing him on the side of his head. Pharaoh wasn't as tall as Bash so it was easier to knock him out.

"Aye, watch your hands."

"Typical Yah-Yah," Kesh mouthed.

"Bitch, not today. I'm due at any time but you can get your ass drug at any time too. I'm not talking to you, I'm talking to your nigga," I told Kesh.

"I dare you to put your damn hands on me. I'll beat that baby outta of your ass."

"Guhhhh, you got one damn tooth in the front of your mouth and if I'm not mistaken, I knocked that bitch out almost a year ago. If you want the other one, step the fuck away from me."

"Kesh, go 'head on. You came and got what you needed for the girls now take your ass on so Yah-Yah and I can have a normal conversation without the arguing and shit," Pharaoh told her.

Kesh looked me up and down before walking off. Pharaoh waited until she was completely gone before he turned his attention back to me.

"Why you coming on the block coming at me like I'm your nigga?"

"Why the hell you telling Bash lies? I've never talked to you 'bout our business."

"Nigga should not have answered your phone."

"I told your ass to stop hitting me up, anyway."

"Yah-Yah, I'm not trying to break up y'all lil' shit. Your nigga ain't gon' punk me though. If he feels like we got pressure, then we will handle it when we see each other. Me and you are trying to be friends, I don't give a fuck 'bout that nigga and how he feels."

"After today, don't say shit else to me. You started some shit that didn't need to even be started. I tried to be nice to you but it ain't working."

"Damn, my bad, Yah-Yah. I didn't think it was a big deal. I wasn't expecting that nigga to answer your phone. Shit, I thought y'all wasn't together. If I knew he was 'round you, I wouldn't have called your ass. The only reason I called was to tell you I dropped off the gifts for your baby with the doorman."

"Okay, well let's just end this whole friendship shit right now. I appreciate you for the gifts but don't call or text me anymore."

"If that's what you want, then cool."

"Cool," I said walking off.

By the time I made it back to my car, my back was hurting and I was out of breath. I was out here acting a fool when I was due at any moment. The thing was, I didn't need Bash mad with me. I wanted to be the only one mad and now with him knowing me and Pharaoh talked, it added more friction to our broken relationship. Before going home, I went and spent the money for a new phone. This was my first child and I didn't know what to expect.

Just like Pharaoh said, he left the packages with my doorman. He was nice enough to bring them up for me. Neca has my baby's room looking like a pink palace. She made everything a unicorn theme and it was gorgeous. During my down time, I managed to make my daughter her first outfit to wear home with a matching headband. Without opening the boxes Pharaoh dropped off, I just dragged them into the baby's room.

As I showered, I thought about Bash and the look in his eyes when he found out I had been talking to Pharaoh. He was hurt but he was taking it way out of hand. The most we talked about was how I was feeling that day and had I ate. It was never anything sexual or about us getting back together. I wanted to call and explain it to him but was afraid he would ignore my calls. The way he fucked my phone up, I'm sure if I wasn't pregnant he would've killed me. Picking my phone up, I dialed his number anyway.

"Are you in labor?" He asked as soon as he picked up the phone.

"No, well...I'm having small contractions but-."

"What you want then?"

I pulled the phone away from ear to get myself together because I didn't want to argue but hearing Esha's voice in the background was all I needed.

"I guess you staying home tonight which is why you rushing me off the phone," I told him.

"I told you not to call me anyway so you heard what you ain't have no business hearing."

"Wow! So you were just begging me but now you back home. I swear you ain't shit and I was calling to explain myself and apologize."

"You ain't got to apologize for shit. Gon' on back to your nigga. Just make sure not to have my daughter 'round him and my threat still remains so I advise you to keep your legs closed while carrying her."

"Who the fuck do you think I am? I wasn't a hoe when we met and I'm not one now. But I'll open my legs all I want. Ain't nobody stopping you from sticking your dick in your baby mama."

"I'm single, my dick is free game right now. I can fuck a million bitches if I wanted to."

The tears started stinging my eyes with every word that he said. It was always crazy to me how a man will be ready to kill you if he thinks you gave another nigga some pussy but when he do it, it's cool.

"Just call me when you go in labor," he said before disconnecting the call.

"Fuck you, Bash!" I screamed, slamming my phone down on my dresser.

He proved to me tonight exactly why I wasn't in a hurry to take him back. When he's mad at me, he runs home to her so she can soothe something only I can do. It was time for me to really move on and let this shit go for good. My birthday was about a week away, and I was hoping she would come before then. Shutting off the lights, I climbed in the bed and was sleep before I could count to ten.

~

BIRTHDAY...

Here I was barely able to walk as Neca dragged me through the mall hoping the walking would send me into labor. As much as I was huffing and puffing, you would think she was about to fall out. The doctor told me she was very stubborn and when she was ready, she would make her appearance. Even while big as a house, I was still cute and made sure I looked decent. Neca wouldn't let me slip if I wanted to. She had my hair flat-ironed out and it was touching the middle of my back. Thanks to my daughter, my hair was at its healthiest.

"Oh shit...oh shit...oh shit," Neca stated, trying to turn me in another direction.

"What is it? Why the hell you yanking me?"

"Bash, guh, and he's not alone," she said lowly.

Bash was heading towards us with E'shon in his arms and Esha walking on the other side of him with a handful of bags. I should've walked away but my feet were stuck. He needed to know that I saw his ass being a little family man. Neca could feel the heat radiating from my body so she tried to soften the introduction once they got closer.

"What's up Bash?" Neca spoke.

E'shon immediately started whining and reaching for me but today, I wasn't going to touch him. He was with both of his biological parents and there was no need for me to keep getting attached to him knowing I would never be a part of his life like that.

"What's up. Y'all doing a little shopping?" He asked, undressing me with his eyes. He was so into me that Esha had to slightly bump him to bring his attention back.

"Yea, just getting Yah-Yah out the house so she can have this baby and it's my girl birthday so I decided to spend some money on her for her after baby body."

"Yea? I forgot today was your birthday. Well y'all hit me up when she ready." He adjusted E'shon in his arms and walked off with Esha following.

The feeling of fluid running down my leg reminded me I wasn't dreaming that my man was with his family and ignoring me like I wasn't standing here. The long dress I had on covered what was going on between my legs.

"Neca, I think my water just broke."

"Bitch what? Let me go get Bash!"

"No! Please just get me to the hospital. There's no way I'm gon' make it home and have time for them to set up all that shit."

"But you don't want him..." her voice trailed off after I gave her a look.

"Fuck him, he got who he wants. I'll take care of my baby on my own. If I feel like it, I'll call him once she gets here."

Right before midnight my daughter came into the world screaming. It felt so good to share a birthday with her. She came out with the prettiest black curly hair and deep dark eyes. Her skin was like a Hershey bar and her legs were long just like Bash's. When they laid her on my chest, I thought I would never stop crying. Big Ma and Neca snapped pictures and comforted me as they finished doing whatever they were doing between my legs. My daughter ended up weighing nine pounds even. She was so big that if I hadn't pushed her out within the last hour, I was going into surgery.

Kai Rose was the spitting image of Bash. As she nursed, I stared down at her contemplating if I should call him or not. Of course Big Ma told me I should and Neca said it didn't matter. It had been a whole day since I had her and I was going home tomorrow. I wasn't that bitter that I would keep him away from her. As she continued to nurse, I sent him a picture instead of calling. Less than a minute, my phone notified me of a message.

Bash: So you have her and not call me so I could experience the shit? I swear you starting to irk me more and more.

Me: Letting you know was definitely a mistake. I don't want to get on your nerves so just lose my number.

A few minutes went by before he texted back.

Bash: I'm on the way. Text me the room number.

I texted Bash the room number and waited for him to arrive. Yesterday was such a blur that what I thought was my worse birthday ended up being the best birthday I ever had. It was going to take Bash a little while to get here if he was at his house so I got Kai changed and into a fresh one-piece before he got there. For my sanity, I hoped he wouldn't come in here with an attitude. He made it clear that we were through and went back to Esha and I had no choice but to respect it.

"Hey, I got some more flowers for you," the nurse said.

"You can sit them down over by the other ones."

My room was full of balloons, flowers and gifts. Most of them came from clients and Neca. I had her take Big Ma home so she could rest. Neither of them wanted to leave but there was no need to sit up here with me. I was going to need all the help I could get when I went home tomorrow. The nurse sat the flowers down and walked out the room. Laying Kai down, I went to read the card that was attached.

Congratulations on the new baby. I'm here if you need anything.

~Pharaoh

Bash walked in as I was sticking the card back into the flowers. Without acknowledging him, I got back in the bed and focused my attention on the television. It wasn't shit on that I was interested in but it was helping me keep my eyes off of him. He went from looking grungy looking from me not fucking with him, back to his normal sexy self. Esha must be putting it on his ass. Out of my peripheral I could see him sanitize his hands before he placed a blanket over his shirt and picked Kai up. I finally looked at him to see his reaction. He stared at her and placed a kiss on her forehead before placing her on his chest.

"You named her Kai Rose? Why Rose?" He asked, quickly looking at me and back at her.

"It's my mama middle name."

"Oh, that's cool. Did you give her my last name?"

"No, I gave her mine."

Bash squeezed the bridge of his nose and let out a sigh. I did think about it but figured it was best for her to have my last name and if Bash wanted it changed then we would cross that bridge.

"Why the hell would you give my child your name? That's childish as fuck, Yahria."

"Nigga, I don't know if you gon' be in her life or not. I did what I thought was best. Now if you want the name changed go talk to the damn nurse before they turn the bitch in. I don't give a fuck either way it go. The last thing I want is to be childish or irk your nerves like you said earlier. I'm not trying to be a bitch but you won't have to worry 'bout me calling you for shit."

"You sound crazy."

"Nah, I sound real. If you want to do for her then just do it but don't expect me to call you."

"Where all this coming from? I said you irked me 'cause your ass could've called me and told me you were in labor."

"I went in labor right after you walked away from me with Esha at the mall. Neca wanted to run and get you but I told her not to interrupt you and your family. Shit, I'm the outsider so I'm playing my position as baby mama. Since you back with Esha, I'm sure you'll go 'head and marry her now."

"Who the hell said I was back with Esha? Did you hear me say that? Damn, you always assuming something. That shit aggravating as fuck, too."

"What you expect me to think if you're over there and you 'round her all the time. Just like we not together but every time we 'round each other our feelings get the best of us," I told him.

"We both made it clear we were through so I'm free to do me and you free to do you. All we got between us is our daughter. I've came to the conclusion that we ain't meant to be together and I should've never pursued you."

I swallowed the dry lump in my throat. In so many words he was telling me that our whole relationship should have never happened. He would say all of this after I carried his child for nine months and went through pure hell with his damn mama. My emotions were about to get the best of me. Instead of slapping the shit out of him, I got up and got me some clean clothes so I could take a shower. Behind the closed door with the shower on, I broke down crying. Bash did something to me because I never did this much crying with Pharaoh. He made me soft and it was time for me to turn my savage back on.

The shower was just what I needed to make me feel better. My blow out was now frizzy so I pulled all my hair up in a ball on top of my head until I got home tomorrow. Stepping out of the bathroom and back in the room, Bash was laying in my bed with his shirt off and Kai had on nothing but a diaper laying on his chest.

"Why are y'all half naked?"

"The nurse told me to give her skin to skin contact. You were in the bathroom so damn long and she started wanting breast milk I guess. The nurse came in and helped me get her soothed. She said you need to pump some milk, too," he said looking me over.

"Okay, well can you get out of my bed. I'm the one that birth a big ass baby, not you."

"She's perfect, Yahria. I know we argue and shit but I'm glad the both of you are okay. It means a lot to me that you birth me a little girl."

"Yea, you welcome."

Bash gave Kai over to me and I got her dressed so I could feed her again. She ate so much that she was damn near connected to me constantly. She was starting to make me regret to agreeing to breast-feed. Bash stood over me as I pulled my breasts out so she could latch on. She finally popped her eyes open once that milk hit her tongue and Bash was able to see her fully.

"Wow! She is really beautiful. I ain't gon' never have any money," Bash said.

As he stood over me staring at her, I did my best to ignore him and prayed he went home after I was done but he didn't. It was almost eight at night and he was still sitting in the rocking chair holding her. It did allow me to take a nap peacefully.

"You better get going before Esha start worrying 'bout you," I told him.

"Why you worried 'bout what she thinks? I'm spending time with my child. You rushing me off so your nigga can come up here and bring you some more flowers?"

I laughed because for him not to want me, he was all in my shit being nosey. He got up from the chair and laid Kai down. I adjusted in the bed because he was finally about to take his ass home so I

could go back to sleep. Bash walked over to the bed and pulled me by
my shirt so I was face to face with him.

"You laughing like this shit funny. I never cheated on your young
ass but clearly your ass out here fuckin' if he sending gifts to my
daughter and flowers. How the nigga know you had the baby
anyway?"

"First of all, let me the fuck go before I knock the fuck outta you
and second, I posted her picture on my social media." Bash loosened
his grip but he didn't let me go.

"You going back to that nigga, ain't you?"

"At this point, I don't think it matters. We both single, right? I may
fuck him a few times or let him eat me out. It depends on what mood
I'm in," I smiled at him.

Bash yanked me so hard I'm sure my brain shifted.

"You playing but I'm dead ass serious right now. You fuck him and
get ready to sign my daughter over 'cause I'm killing both of y'all."

"For what, though? I'm not yours. All you ask is for me not to have
him 'round your daughter. I'll make sure to drop her off with her
step-mama before I go lay-up." I could tell I was starting to get under
his skin. This is what he wanted from me. I was no longer Yahria to
him but I was Yah-Yah again and I didn't give a fuck about his
feelings.

"Let me get the fuck away from you 'cause you acting stupid as
fuck right now," he said, releasing my shirt.

"You can't take the fact that I'm giving you back what you give me.
I know you fucked Esha already and I ain't mad so why you mad
'cause I'm 'gon jump on another nigga dick? You throw up in my face
how we single but you jacking me up like you still want me."

"Maybe I do and you making the shit hard for me."

"Bash take your ass on back home. You want me now 'cause I'm
no longer pregnant and you don't want no one else to have me. I see
this shit all the time which is why I didn't want to have a baby in the
first place but you made a promise to me that you had me. Now look
at this shit," I told him, trying to hold back my tears.

"I never said I didn't have you, Yahria. I'll forever give you and Kai what y'all need but me and you can't seem to figure out what we want to do so I came to the conclusion that we need to officially end this shit with each other. Hell yea, I'm gon' be mad knowing that you giving another nigga something that should be mine. That's what happens when you love someone but you can't have them."

"Everything I said was out of hurt and anger. You'll never understand how I feel and I don't expect you to. Do I want you to be with Esha, no! But I have to accept the fact that you picked her and not me."

"I didn't pick her. I picked you but you kept brushing me off when I was trying. How long did you want me to try?"

"So, y'all are back together?" I asked him for clarity.

There was a long pause before he stood up from the bed and walked over to wear Kai was laying.

"I really don't call it that but I do stay there a few nights out the week for my son."

I nodded my head to let him know that he gave me just what I needed to know. He walked back over to me and sat closer to me this time.

"I haven't slept with her or touched her since she been back. We talk occasionally and we sleep in separate rooms. She thinks we can make it work and she's willing to be a part of our daughter's life. She's waiting on my answer but I can't give her one right now."

"Why?"

"I'm still in love with you and I can't let you go. It's hard for me to give a woman another chance that purposely left making me think she was dead."

"You think she smart enough to do that by herself?"

"She did it didn't she? For a whole damn year at that."

"Go home and tell her you'll try to work it out with her. Maybe, she had to get away."

I couldn't believe what I was saying. It had to be the medicine in my system because I was being way too nice and just handing Bash over to Esha.

"I know I acted a lil' fucked up yesterday for your birthday but I do have you a gift. I made it a few months ago when I bought the building for you. It may not mean much now but I still want you to have it."

He pulled a box out of his pocket and placed it on my lap. When I opened it I wasn't expecting to see what I saw.

"I got the diamonds imported in, they are very rare and you are the only one in America with them. I was going to ask you to marry me at the reveal party but shit got out of hand. I've carried it 'round with me all this time hoping we could make shit right but maybe this for the best. Promise is still there, I got you with whatever you need but you got to communicate with me and let me know."

"I'm sure I'll be fine, just worry 'bout your daughter."

"I really love you, Yahria, and maybe one day it will go away so it won't hurt every time I got to leave you."

Bash placed a kiss on my lips that ended up being longer than we anticipated. He kissed Kai and was out the door without looking back.

6

E sha

"OOOO SHIT! Yea, stay right there! I'm about to cum." My phone was ringing but I was in the process of getting licked and sucked like a damn popsicle.

"You can answer your phone while I finish you off?"

"I can't...oh my gawd." I arched my back as the wave shot through my body. I never thought this moment would come. It's been over a year since I came so hard and my body was enjoying the euphoric feeling when my phone started ringing again.

"Hello," I said out of breath.

"Where the fuck you at and you know I got to go to work?" Bash's voice boomed through the phone.

I quickly looked at the time on the clock and jumped up from the bed.

"I'm on the way. I lost track of time," I lied.

"Hurry the fuck up," he said before hanging up.

"He sound mad as hell," Kesh said wiping my juices from her mouth.

"He'll be fine. I'll call you when I get home," I pecked her on her lips and stuck my panties in my purse.

Kesh and I became close once I found out about Bash and Yahria. We hung out whenever I could break away from Kelly and my crybaby ass son. Bash and I were trying to work it out but he was always angry and he would never hold a conversation with me. As soon as he went to bed, I slipped out of the house and came over here with Kesh. We started drinking and watching movies until we fell asleep. This morning, I woke up with her in between my legs playing with my clit.

Kesh would always talk about being with women but I wasn't interested. She showed me something different and I was loving it. I was already planning my next escape so she could make me feel like she just did. Her children were with their dad for the week so the anticipation of me coming back tonight was killing me. Pulling back up to the house almost an hour later, I checked my hair to make sure I wasn't looking like I had been out all night. Kelly was here so I was confused on why he called me to come home.

"Listen, I don't give a fuck what you do 'round this bitch but have your ass here when it's time to take care of your child," Bash went in on me before I could get through the door.

"I just ran to get some gas. You know I never leave the house. Is it an issue with me leaving to get gas?"

Bash looked me up and down like he knew I had been out having the best orgasm of my life. He did his thing in the bedroom but it was something about Kesh. She knew my body and how to get it to react to her.

"I don't give a fuck what you do Esha. My only concern is my child and when I'm trying to go to work I need you here with him because it's not my mama responsibility to raise our child. She done enough while your ass was gone getting high," he spewed.

I followed him up the stairs to his bedroom where I still wasn't allowed to sleep. He had a duffle bag on the bed when I entered and I had a feeling he was going over to Yahria's.

"Bash I thought we were working on us? Why are you so angry with me? All I do is sit here and try my best to take care of our son but you give me your ass to kiss. Some days you're warm and the other days you're cold. I can tell the days you haven't talked to your other baby mama because you cold as hell and don't want to be bothered. Is this where you want to be?"

"I'm here ain't I?" He looked over his shoulder as he changed shirts.

His back was so cut up that you would think someone sculpted it personally. Bash was by far one of the sexiest men I had ever laid eyes on. He knew he had the whole package as it pertained to what women wanted and he could have any woman he wanted but he was here with me. His heart was just over at Yahria's house.

"You're here but really you're not. I'm trying to see how we working on us and I can't even sleep in the bed with you. The same bed we made our son in."

"You can sleep in here 'cause I won't be here tonight. I'll be back in a few days."

"Where you going?"

"I'm going to my condo and then I'm going to spend some time with my daughter. Is that a problem?"

"You staying over there with your daughter?"

"Does it matter?"

"Yes it matters if we trying to be together. What happened with you? You never disrespected me or women period."

"I'm not disrespecting you, Esha. We ain't made nothing official yet. I'm still single and trying to figure out if you're worth another shot but you on thin ice."

"How?"

"You left here last night with panties on. They were yellow with black lace, right? You standing here right now with no panties on.

Next time, fix your hair in the back too. I know what a woman looks like when she been fucked good. I been doing it for years."

"I didn't leave last night. I told you, I went and got some gas," I continued lying.

"A'ight Esha. It's cool, we gotta get it from somewhere right?" He looked at me and smirked.

"So you going to fuck your baby mama?"

"I told you I was going to my condo and going to see my daughter. Where me fucking Yahria coming from?"

"That smirk on your face."

"I'm not the one 'round here laying up, you are. Don't try to put the pressure on me 'cause you fuckin' 'round."

Bash grabbed his bag and walked out of the room. Kelly gave him just enough time to leave before she brought her ass in there with E'shon.

"Bitch let me tell you something, if you fuck this up I promise you I'll make sure Bash cut your ass off. If you are fucking you better not get caught with your dumb ass."

"I don't give a damn no more Kelly. I'll just tell him all this shit is your fault. I wouldn't be fighting for his attention if you weren't a jealous ass bitch and tried to kill me. Now this new bitch done had a baby and I can't even get my man's attention. I got needs too."

"I'll handle Yahria. Just keep your damn mouth closed and if I feel like you 'bout to tell Bash that I had something to do with this I'll make sure I kill you myself. Take care of your damn son."

My son started crying as soon as Kelly walked out. I didn't know what I was doing wrong with him but he hated me. He was never satisfied with anything I had done for him. He wouldn't eat, he barely let me change him, and he fought his sleep so bad to the point he would get exhausted and fall asleep playing with his toys. I tried everything to get my own child to like me.

Not being the best cook, I tried to cook me and my son something to eat since we were now in this big ass house by ourselves. He did manage to eat and was now asleep so I had time to see if Kesh was available to hook up again.

"I knew you would be calling me," Kesh said.

"Yea, I was calling to see when can I see you again?"

"I'm free whenever. You know my kids gone."

"Okay, I'm about to send you the address but don't come until tonight. It's just me and my son here but we got to be very careful."

"I know all about being careful. I'll see you tonight."

7

B ash

SINCE YAHRIA HAD THE BABY, I tried to stay away from her but it was hard when we had a new baby together. I made sure I spent time with my daughter at least every other day. Yahria was doing an excellent job with her especially being that she didn't have any help. When I was there, Yahria closed herself up in her room or she spent that time doing laundry or cleaning up. She had a dope little spot not too far from my condo but I wasn't going to tell her that. If she knew, her ass would try to move knowing her. She kept her conversation with me short and she never looked at me.

My daughter was four weeks old now, and she was fat from that breast milk she was drinking. Yahria was looking fine as fuck too. Her stomach was flat and her ass and titties had filled in nicely. She was cooking while I put Kai to sleep. I had been there for over an hour and the most we said was hey to each other. She did ask me was I thirsty but that was it. Yea, I was thirsty but only for her. I had to play it cool, though. She probably was back with Pharaoh and I didn't want to know that right now because there was no telling what I would do.

"How long you gon' be here?" Yahria asked.

"I mean, she sleep now so if you want me to go, I'll go."

"No, I'm 'bout to step out for a little bit and I was just making sure she was straight with you or I could take her to Big Ma."

"Nah, she good with me. I'll chill here until you come back."

"You're welcome to eat if you want to. I shouldn't be gone too long. Kai has milk in the freezer, just take it out and run it under some hot water to make it warm and put it in a bottle."

"A'ight."

Yahria went to her bedroom and closed the door. I turned the channel and slipped my shoes off so I could lay down with Kai. Yahria ended up waking me up before walking out the door. She was dressed nice but not to the point you would think she was going out to be with a nigga. She had her hair down and curly like I liked it and her shoulders were out showing Kai's name in a pretty font. Her jeans were ripped up showing a little thigh meat but that was cool.

"I'll be back in a few hours."

"Ain't it a little too early to be out fuckin'? I thought you had to wait six weeks?" I asked, waiting on her response.

"I'm cleared to fuck if I want but if you must know, I'm not going to fuck anybody. I'm going on a dinner date with a client and Nina that you met at the charity event."

"I mean, I ain't worried 'bout it. I just don't want you out there with the afterbirth smell trying to throw your lil' pussy 'round."

Yahria busted out laughing before grabbing her purse and heading for the door.

"You real pressed 'bout who I give my shit to. You've had your face in my shit since I had your daughter so you know it don't smell like afterbirth. Call me if you need me," she said before walking out the door.

Damn, she put me out there. She was right, I did eat her ass out earlier this week. I was at my condo going through my photos of us until a picture of her pussy popped up. I didn't text her and tell her I was on the way or nothing. I popped up at her spot and snatched her ass up. I ate her on the sofa while my daughter was sleep in the next room. Right after I was done, Yahria put my ass out and here I am two days later in my feelings because she dressed up and going out.

It was time for me to be real with Yahria. I thought I was going to see where me and Esha could go but I couldn't stand to be around her. She was sneaky as fuck, and I couldn't trust her. And it's been months and my son still don't like her ass. The way Yahria been acting lately, I'm not sure if I could handle her rejection. She never asked me for anything but I was always sending shit to her to just let her know she was on my mind. Gifts meant nothing to her because most of them were still in the same package I sent them in unless it was for Kai.

At close to ten at night, Yahria's ass still hadn't made it home. I hadn't tried to call her yet because there was no need to but Kai was on her last bottle and she was going to be raising hell if she didn't have any breast milk. The few hours Yahria lied about ended up being six hours. Making sure not to wake my daughter up, I eased from by her and grabbed my phone to call Yahria. When she picked up the phone, the sound of loud music could be heard in the background.

"You plan on bringing your ass home to your daughter? We are out of milk."

"I lost track of time. I'm on the way," she disconnected the call.

The time alone I spent with Kai was much needed. She had a feisty side to her like her mama but she also had this sweetness to her when she opened her eyes and stared at me. Kai knew exactly who I was when she heard me talking to her. A little before midnight, Yahria walked in the house. I looked her over to see if anything was out of place in her but I came up empty.

"Why the hell you staring at me like that?" Yahria asked.

"I'm not staring at you," I lied. "Did you have fun?"

"Yes, I did. It was nice to get out and talk business for once. I'm ready to get back to work and move on to bigger and better things."

"You don't think you moving too fast? What are your plans for Kai when you go back to work?"

"I'm taking my baby with me and Farah is going to tend to her while I work."

I forgot that I kept Farah on payroll. Once Esha and my mama called themselves taking over my house, Farah moved out when Yahria did. She couldn't stand my mama for some reason and refused to stay. She promised that she would be available for me and Yahria whenever we needed her.

"I can't argue with that," I told her.

Yahria sat down at the other end of the sofa and took her shoes off. The pink polish on her toes made her chocolate skin stand out more. The only thing that our daughter got from her was her dark skin which made her even more beautiful.

"Thank you for watching her for me today. I didn't mean to be out so late but they wanted to go for a few drinks."

"You can't breastfeed my daughter and you been drinking, Yahria."

"Damn, Bash, I know that already. I said they wanted drinks. That doesn't mean I was drinking. Give me more credit than you giving me, damn."

"Where is my baby anyway?"

"She in the room sleep. I fed her, her last bottle about thirty minutes ago and changed her."

"She'll be up in 'bout two hours then. She's like clockwork almost with her feedings. Did you sit here and hold her all day?"

"Kinda. She is going to be a daddy's girl for sure."

"That's good to know. I'm glad she has you in her life."

Yahria smiled at me but that faded when she saw Esha's name come across my screen. She got up and excused herself to give me some privacy.

"What is it?"

"I was calling to see if you were coming home tonight?"

"Nope! I ain't been home in a few weeks now. Do I need to come and get E'shon?"

"No, he went home with your mama and it's just me in this big ass house.," she whined.

"And what you want me to do?"

"I thought maybe you would come home so we could talk about us and see where it goes from there."

Yahria reappeared in a nice short one-piece pajama set that showed her pussy print. I forgot I was on the phone because my dick was jumping in my damn jeans.

"Did you hear me."

"Yea...I mean nah! I'll go by my mama house and get him. I'll holla at you later," I hung up in her face.

"Come here, Yahria," I called out to her.

"What you want?" She stood in the kitchen putting the leftovers away.

Her apartment was small but it fit her perfectly. Everything was open until you went down the hall to the bedrooms and bathroom.

"Come here," I told her again.

This girl was so sexy and she wasn't even trying. I wanted her so bad and she wanted me too or she wouldn't have went and put this little shit on to get my attention. Then I thought about it; Yahria always wore some little shit to bed. Because it was so late, I was able to see her change because I was usually gone by now. Yahria came and stood in front of me so I pulled her in closer until my face was leveled with her stomach.

"Why you acting like you're not familiar with me. I know every-thing 'bout your body. I smell her sweetness already." I caressed her hips and ass. "Come sit down on my lap."

"Bash, I'm not 'bout to go there with you. If I let you do this then what?"

"It's whatever you want it to be. I'm going off your vibe. You know where I stand, though."

"Last I heard you were playing house with your fiancé,"

"Man, come sit your ass down before Kai wake up." I grabbed her little ass and forced her down on my lap.

My dick was so hard that if I didn't let it out of my jeans and briefs it was going to explode. I hadn't touched Yahria like this in months and I missed it. Her skin was so soft and she smelled so good. I brought her face to mine and kissed her. She was hesitant at first so I started kissing her neck as I unbuttoned the front of her one piece.

"Yahria, can I make love to you? I miss you so much."

"Bash, I don't think we should do this."

"Tell me why?"

"The only thing that's going to come from this is more hurt feelings. I can't take anything else, Bash."

"I'm not going to let anyone hurt you. Baby, just please let me do this. I need you so bad," I said, softly kissing on her breast.

That was one of her weak spots and I knew if I could just get her in the moment, I would have her ass folded up like a pretzel, sliding my dick in and out of her wetness. The moan that escaped her mouth was all I needed to take this shit to another level. She had already soaked up her one piece so I made her take it off. My mouth watered looking at her stand before with nothing on. I could tell she had just given birth due to the dark line going down the middle of her stomach. I unzipped my jeans and pulled them off. My dick was standing straight up to the ceiling. Yahria licked her lips but quickly acted like she wasn't looking at it.

"Come bend your ass over on this sofa," I told her.

Yahria didn't hesitate to do what I told her. I spread her ass cheeks and placed my face right in her ass. Taking my time, I licked her from her clit to her ass until she was spitting her juice all down my throat. She had my face soaking wet to the point the shit was dripping from my beard. I sat down and slapped her on her ass. She knew exactly what to do.

"We need a condom," she stated.

"If you don't come and sit your ass down on my dick I know something. My shit hard as a damn brick to the point that bitch hurt and you talking 'bout a condom. You should've been saying that before that lil' girl got here."

"I don't know, Bash. If you been sleeping with her I don't want to catch nothing. She was missing for a year," she reminded me.

"Yahria, I ain't slept with her. You are the last person I slept with. I been jacking my dick so much me and my hand got carpal tunnel in it."

It felt good to get a laugh out of her. The friction between us was wearing me out and as much as I said I didn't want to be with her my heart wouldn't let me move on. I tried to stay mad at her so I wouldn't think about her but I always ended up falling deeper for her.

"Come on, damn," I told her.

Yahria finally moved and straddled me. My head touched her wetness and made me squeeze the base of my dick to hold my nut. It was so hot and tight that I had to close my eyes and think about something that would stop me from nutting. I was able to get about five pumps before Kai started crying over the baby monitor.

"Shit, let me get this one. It won't take me long; it's right there. Just squeeze that shit like I taught you."

"No, Bash! Let me go get her. She doesn't usually wake up for at least another hour."

"She blocking me from getting some pussy is what she doing."

"If it's meant to be you'll get it."

"You damn right I'm gon' get it. Right after you put her back to sleep so hurry the hell up."

Yahria took so long I ended up falling asleep waiting on her. When I woke up and walked to her room she was in the bed sleep with Kai sleeping right up under her. I didn't even bother her, I put my briefs back on and got in the bed with them. This was how my life was supposed to be; the only person missing was my son.

"Bash! Get up," Yahria fussed.

"Damn, What?"

"I know you hear Kai screaming next to you."

I was sleeping so hard I didn't hear her.

"She just showing out 'cause she can't feel nobody."

As soon as I grabbed her and put her on my chest she calmed down.

"You plan on going home today?" Yahria asked, drying off.

"Why you rushing me out of here? You got somebody coming over?"

"No, I'm just asking 'cause you got another family to tend to and you can't do it from here."

"My son is with my mama but I'm 'bout to go get him after we finish doing what we started last night."

"Nope! You are not 'bout to get me jammed up again. For one, I'm not on any birth control 'cause I didn't plan on sleeping 'round with nobody. Second, you not 'bout to get my feelings involved with you and then you get pissed with me and take your ass back over there to her. I'm not doing the back and forth shit with you."

"Here you go. I'm trying to fix what me and you had. Do I need to spell it out for you? I, Bash, want you, Yahria. I gave you a ring that I personally made for you and gave you this beautiful lil' girl. What else you want and need Yahria?"

Yahria leaned up against the dresser and looked at me. I could tell she was thinking about what I said to her. She was stubborn and it wasn't going to be easy to show her that it was her that I wanted.

"We can start by at least trying to communicate with each other again. But a relationship right now is on hold until I see you got your affairs in order. I'm not the one with the issues that need to be resolved so once I see you got that under control then we can talk 'bout me and you again."

"I can dig that. We have been being a lil' rough with each other lately."

"Yea, I try to avoid you 'cause my mouth don't have a filter and you been a lil' mouthy too."

"Mouthy?"

"Yea, you been saying some flaw shit too. The only person that should be mad is me."

"So, what you gon' do 'bout your homie, lover, friend Pharaoh?"

"Why you so worried 'bout him? He not worried 'bout you."

"Yahria, don't make me fuck you up."

"For what?"

"You not 'bout to have your cake and eat it too."

"Neither are you but we not together so you can't tell me who to cut off. Get your shit together and then I'll solely focus on you."

I chilled with them for a few hours before I went to get my son from my mama. From the time she let me in the house, I knew something was off with her. She was never the junkie type but the house was a mess. She had laundry piled up in the laundry room. She let E'shon tear up the living room.

"You alright?" I asked her.

"You smell just like her. Just can't let her go can you, son? You got the woman you love at home in that big ass house by herself while you go lay up with Yahria. What has she done for you besides give you a child?"

"Ma, let me ask you this. What the fuck you got against Yahria? What if I don't want Esha trifling ass, then what?"

"Then you a damn fool. Esha has always had your best interest at heart. Yahria don't want you; she wants what you can do for her."

"Yahria ain't asked me for shit. Everything I've ever done for her was 'cause I wanted to, not 'cause she had her hand out."

"I hope nothing ever happens to your precious little Yahria. I hate to be the one to pick you up again."

"As long as I'm breathing no one would ever be able to hurt a hair on her head."

"Be careful with what you say, son."

"You be careful with what you say, ma."

I grabbed my son and left out. She could sit her ass in the house miserable and bitter. I didn't give a fuck about what she thought about Yahria anymore. Esha was about to get her a piece of my mind as soon as I got back to the house.

8

Yah-Yah

"YOU BETTER KNOW WHAT YOU DOING," Big Ma said as I took Kai out the car seat and handed her over.

"Stop acting like we sleeping together. He's been a real good friend to me through this whole thing."

"He still loves you Yah-Yah. What you gon' do with two men in love with you? Somebody gon' end up getting fucked up."

"I'm not giving him mixed signals. We are going to lunch together that's it. Why do you like Bash so much?"

"He's the best thing that ever happened to you. Look at you, you look good and I don't have to worry 'bout you in the streets fighting."

"So, that's the reason you let him sleep on your sofa right after he broke my heart?"

"I got a feeling he didn't know what the hell was going on. But what I do know is that his bitch ass mama had something to do with it."

"You think so?"

"The look in that hoe eyes when she came in that reveal party told it all. You make sure you watch her ass."

"We can't be 'round each other so I'm good."

"This Kelly we talking 'bout so like I said, be careful."

"Yes ma'am. I'll be back in a few."

Pharaoh was waiting on me when I pulled up to the Italian spot we liked to eat lunch at. It was something we did at least once a week and I didn't see any harm in it. Pharaoh had really matured since he had his second child. Today, I was meeting his daughter Cissy for the first time. I agreed to meet her because she kept asking about me, I just hope that Pharaoh made it clear that we were not together.

"You looking good, girl," he greeted me with a kiss on my cheek.

"Thank you."

He pulled my chair out for me to sit down. His daughter was seated directly across from me. She was the spitting image of her daddy but you could see Kesh features as well.

"She is pretty daddy," his daughter stated.

"Thank you and you're pretty too," I told her.

"Thank you for meeting us today. Cissy kept hounding me 'bout meeting you so here she is."

"It's nice to meet you. Your daddy talks 'bout you and your sister all the time."

"He talks about you all the time too," she said.

I looked at Pharaoh and he shrugged.

"Are you and my daddy going to get back together? He really needs someone to help him with us."

"Raoh, I thought we had this talk already," I said between clenched teeth.

"She knows we are not together 'cause I messed up."

"Did you put her up to this?"

"Nah!"

"Cissy, me and your daddy are just friends. I have my own daughter as well and I'm trying to figure out how to be a mom myself. I definitely don't want to come into a relationship with my own problems. I'm sure your daddy will find the perfect woman that will love y'all like she's your mom," I told her.

"Yes ma'am," she replied sadly.

I was not about to let this little girl pull on my heart strings to get back with her daddy. It would be wrong of me to even think of having a relationship with Pharaoh knowing I wasn't in love with him and probably never would be again.

"Well, would you look at this shit here," Kelly bopped her handicap ass over to our table.

Without saying a word to her, I placed my napkin in the table and got up from my chair so I could leave. As much as I wanted to beat the fuck out of her, Kai's beautiful face flashed before my eyes.

"No need to leave, Yahria. I'm sure Pharaoh is enjoying your company. Does my son know you're sitting here in your ex face smiling and shit? And where is my granddaughter?"

"Bitch, get the fuck outta my face asking me questions. You know I'm not supposed to be 'round you or I'll be back in jail. As far as me and your son go, that's our muthafuckin' business, not yours. That's the reason we not together now 'cause you always in our business."

"I'm sure he wouldn't like your hoe ass being here with him."

"Kelly, take your dumb ass on somewhere. Every time I see you, you starting some shit with somebody."

I looked between the both of them and thought about how he had just said her name. I never told Pharaoh about Kelly. One thing I never did when I was with Pharaoh, was talk about Bash because that was between me and Bash. The way Kelly was coming at me like I was sitting at the table with her nigga or something.

"Y'all know each other?" I asked them.

"Nah, I don't know this hoe," Pharaoh stated.

"You don't know me, Pharoah? Well, I think it's time to spill a little tea to you, Yahria, since you think you better than me. I been fucking Pharaoh since he been home. I helped his ass get out of jail so he could help me get you away from my son but he was still in love with your ugly ass so I had to pull him away from the plan."

"Is she serious, Pharaoh? And if you lie to me, I swear I will show the fuck out in here and beat your ass," I told him.

"No need to ask him for truth 'cause I got all the truth you need."

Kelly pulled an envelope out her purse and out of it fell a positive pregnancy test and some pictures of her and Pharaoh at her house, at Bash house and several hotels. It pissed me off to see that Pharaoh stumped this low to get me back. I didn't give a fuck about them fucking each other.

"Cissy, it was nice to meet you. Don't you ever in your life date a man like your daddy. Always make sure he treats you like a queen and the first time he shows signs of a fuck nigga, get out," I told her. "As for you, Pharaoh, I don't care 'bout you fuckin' this bitch. She a nasty hoe anyway that wants every damn thing I got. Don't call me, don't text me and don't hit me up in my damn DM's with that begging shit 'cause I don't want to hear it."

"You know this bitch 'bout that drama," Pharaoh stated.

"I don't care, Pharaoh. Just worry 'bout taking care of another baby with this hoe. I hope she makes your life as miserable as she's made mine."

Kelly stood in the way smiling at me as I tried to walk away. For a split second, I wanted to punch her dead in her damn mouth and get the satisfaction of watching her spit her teeth out but I couldn't go to jail right now.

"Move, bitch!" I slightly touched her with my shoulder as I walked out the restaurant.

I got in my car and rushed my ass back to Big Ma house so I could pour this tea while it was hot. My worse fear was Bash being there when I got there. I didn't have to lie about where I was because we weren't official yet but I couldn't tell him his mama was pregnant by my ex nigga either. Bash would probably snap and then I would have to explain why I was with Pharaoh in the first place. I just wasn't in the mood for explaining right now. Bash was feeding Kai when I walked in the house. Big Ma was in the kitchen cooking and running her mouth on the phone as usual. She was used to Bash now that he was just like family. Pharaoh never got to see this side of Big Ma because she never liked him.

"Where you been?" He asked without looking up from Kai.

"Out," I replied, placing my purse down and sitting down next to him.

"Out with Pharaoh?"

"Why?"

"'Cause you left my daughter here to go be with another nigga."

"Boy, bye, if I was with him, it don't matter. You said not to have your child 'round him so I didn't take her. What's your issue? We are not together."

"Yahria, I need you to cut that nigga off completely if you gon' fuck with me. You don't see me running back and forth with you and Esha. I'm trying to show you I want to be with you so I'm doing my part but you on the other hand can't seem to stay your ass away from him. Y'all fuckin' again? Is that why you won't let me get it?"

"No, I'm not fuckin' him and I won't let you get it 'cause I'm not on birth control and I don't want no more damn kids. Why you here anyway?"

"I called your phone but you didn't answer so I called Big Ma and she told me you weren't here but Kai was so I came over here to spend time with her."

"But you were just with her."

"And?"

"Never mind. Hand her here so I can finish feeding her off of one of my breasts 'cause my shit hurting."

"Nope, I hope them bitches get rock hard and have your ass crying tonight. She gon' finish this bottle, I'm gon' burp her and y'all gon' take y'all ass home where you should be unless you working."

"Who the fuck you think you talking to? You don't dictate what I do. Until my last name changes, you can forget thinking you gon' tell me what to do."

"You heard what the fuck I said."

I waved his ass off and went into the kitchen to see what Big Ma was doing. Bash was on some bull and I wasn't in the mood. From the mess I just witness with his mama and Pharaoh the last thing I feel like going through is fussing with him about staying in the house because he wants me all to himself. He was way too blind to realize that he already had me.

"Did you tell him where I was?" I whispered to Big Ma when I got in the kitchen.

"Guh, what I look like? I ain't never been a snitch, nigga. Your ass know that man got GPS in your pussy so get out my face with it."

"I'm sorry, I'm just super stressed right now."

"Well, I advise you to go home and let my grandson in law spread you eagle so you can release that shit so you won't come at me no more. Next time, I'm gon' cut you."

"You won't hurt me," I laughed.

"Oh, Yah-Yah...I got a call from your mama."

My heart started beating a little fast because I had just pulled all of the letters out of my closet and sat them on the bed to start reading them. What could the news be now?

"What is it now?"

"She wants to see you."

"Nah, I'm not 'bout to put myself through that shit with her. It's been years and I don't feel like dealing with her sitting there lying to me 'bout why she did what she did. The answer is no."

"She did everything to take care of you. Your daddy walked out on y'all long before you were born so she was being a mom and did what she had to do to bring some money in the house. I will not allow you to stand your lil' ass here and act like my daughter didn't at least try. 'Cause dammit she did and all I ask is you go see what the hell she want before she dies in that damn place. She begs me all the time to tell you how much she loves you and how proud she is of you. Now you take your ass home and you think 'bout what the hell I said."

I stomped out of the kitchen like a toddler and started snatching all my shit up.

"Put my baby in her seat and bring her to the car, now!" I told Bash as I pushed the door open and walked out.

Why couldn't nobody respect the fact that I didn't want to see my mama. I was just getting to the point I was about to crack one of her letters open. As far as I know, she was in the streets doing her thing while I spent most of my time with Big Ma. I would see her twice a week and that was for her to wash her ass and she was back out the damn door. She was never at any of my school events, no teacher conferences and she wasn't there when I started my period. Why when I finally got my life together, she wants to be in my life?

"I'll be over there in a few. I'm going to get E'shon from his mama."

"Don't worry 'bout coming over. I need to be by myself right now."

"Are you sure? You sound like you need some time alone so who gon' take care of Kai while you waddling in your sorrow?" Bash asked.

"I'm not waddling in shit. Get the hell away from my car," I told him.

He closed the door without saying anything else and I pulled away from Big Ma house. It was like Neca knew when to call to calm me down. I hit the green button on my steering wheel to answer the phone.

"Hello."

"Guh, why I just saw Pharaoh jacking Kelly ass up in the back of his car?"

"It's a long story girl. It's been a long ass day and it just got worse."

"What the hell happened now? Shit, I got time."

"Well, I went to eat lunch with Pharaoh and his daughter and Kelly bring her ass in there on some check a bitch shit. When I heard Pharaoh call her by her first name, I knew something was up. Do you know she got this man out of jail to blackmail me but the shit fell through?"

"Guh, I know you fuckin' lyin'."

"Here's the kicker, they been fuckin' and her old ass pregnant by him."

"Bitch, get off my phone. This tea so damn hot my lips and shit just got scorched."

"Yea, so I told his ass don't fuckin' bother me anymore. That really did it for me. If he loved me, he should have never sided with that bitch. Now I know why his ass was telling me to watch out for her. He knew that bitch had it out for me. She had something to do with Esha's ass popping back up. I just know it."

"Oh, I know that hoe had something to do with it but how did she pull that off?"

"Kelly can pull off anything. She got the money to do what she pleases."

"You got a point."

"Well, the other part of my day is my damn mama wanting to see me and Big Ma cussin' my ass out cause I told her no."

"Yah-Yah, it's time to talk to her don't you think?"

"Hell no, it's not time. I'm mad as hell with her and whoever the hell my daddy is. You don't just leave your child."

"I think she did what she thought was best but hell, what do I know? I think you should talk to her and if I have to go with you, I will."

"I'll let you know. I'm just not even in the mood to think about it right now."

"Think 'bout it and let me know. You know I'm here for you either way it go. I gotta go though 'cause Gip waiting on me downstairs."

"Well, damn! I'm happy for y'all though."

"Bitch, what you happy for? We don't go together. We just kicking it."

"That's some weird kicking it but whatever. I'll call you later."

"A'ight girl."

I got home and got Kai settled in her bed as I looked at the letters on my bed. If I was going to see to her, I needed to read these letters and see what she was talking about all this time. It was going to take me weeks to read all these letters but it had to be done.

9

K elly

I STAYED AWAY from Bash and Esha's house until my black eye healed. Now, yes Pharaoh was wrong as hell for putting his hands on me but to be honest, I punched his ass so hard that he saw stars so I kind of deserved it. What really set him off was I did it in front of his daughter. Before I could apologize he had my ass hemmed up on the back of his car slapping the shit out of me. Things got out of hand and I was now able to come out of the house and go check on Esha. She called me and told me that Bash was coming to talk to her but she didn't know why. I hoped for her sake she didn't get caught sleeping with that damn girl.

Esha opened the door once I got there. She seemed to be happy. The house was spotless and she even attempted to cook something. One thing I did notice was her pants were starting to fall off of her. I put it on Bash stressing her out because she was still pretty thick everywhere else. She sat down on the sofa in the den and grabbed her phone like I wasn't there to see what the hell was going on with them.

"Heifer, I know damn well you not just gon' ignore me. What the hell going on?"

"I think Bash is coming to tell me he done. He ain't stayed here in forever. He rarely brings E'shon home anymore and I'm tired of hiding my feelings that I have for Kesh."

"Kesh," I huffed. "Bitch you just as confused as she is. Both of y'all hoes fuckin' each other 'cause the men y'all want don't want y'all ass. If you feel like it's love, then cool but both of y'all dumb as fuck to me. When did Bash say he was coming?"

"He told me he was coming but that was about three hours ago."

"I'll stay here until he comes. He won't be able to break shit off as long as I'm here."

"Kelly, why you just won't leave this shit alone? He don't want me and I don't want him. I thought I did but not with Kesh in my life, I'm good."

"I'll leave it alone once Yahria is gone for good."

"Why do you hate her? She's never done anything to me and she loves my son unconditionally. Who wouldn't want a woman like her in their life? Evidently, she keeps Bash happy."

"I'm supposed to make my son happy!" I yelled at her. "From the time he was old enough to start dating I would sabotage every fuckin' girl that thought she was going to get a piece of my son. I had bitches lined up to date him and I shut all that shit down. A few slid under my nose but it was just a quick fuck and he was done with them by the time I got in his head. I eliminate all his problems, that includes you and Yahria."

"You are sounding crazy right now."

"Bitch, you ain't seen crazy. After you get my son back with you I want you to get him as far away from here as possible. I'll pay for it."

"Kelly, how? How am I supposed to get him to want me? I've tried everything."

"Everything but sucking his dick," I told her.

"Kelly?"

"Don't *Kelly* me. Bitch, if you don't get on your knees when he walks through that door and handle your business he will never want you back. Yahria just had a baby so I know he's not getting it there. I'll stay in my room. If that doesn't work, then I'll intervene. Go get yourself together so you'll be ready when he comes home."

Esha got up to head up the stairs. From the look on her face, I could tell she was still unsure.

"Damn, I got to teach y'all young girls every damn thing," I said walking in the kitchen to get something to drink.

While I was helping her with her problems, I was trying to figure out how long I was going to hide this baby. I was over fifty and there was no way this baby was going to be healthy but I didn't want to get rid of it because it was my way of holding onto Pharaoh. I saw how he cared for his children and I loved it. I even paid attention to how he treated Kesh now.

People could call me jealous all they wanted to but only I knew the deep root of this shit. For years, I've held in everyone's secrets and held up an image to keep everyone safe but I was about to explode. There was a hate that I had for my son. I know, that was mean, right? But you have to understand why I feel this way. I was never supposed to have kids. To be honest, I never wanted them because of the responsibility. Subashtian turned out to be a pretty good child but I still hated him because he looked just like his daddy. I wanted Subashtian's daddy all to myself but he was married so I shared him.

It started out as a get-back thing that turned into lust, then love. He loved me more than he loved his wife but he was invested into his marriage. I was married too but my husband was doing so much traveling that we didn't have much time for each other so I slipped in my brother in laws bed and slept with him at least two or three days a week. We pretended that nothing was going on between us for years until my sister starting getting the big head with her job. He started getting messy when he noticed she wasn't going to help him get promoted.

We slept together for several years, even after Subashtian was born. My sister still doesn't have a clue that my son is also her stepson. It was a secret that I was taking to my grave because it would kill her. She thought she was better than me anyway. I held the power in my hand to crush my sister and my son's world. I loved Subashtian but I feel like he ruined my life and he owed me. He couldn't take care of me if he kept having kids with these hoes. I accepted E'shon but Yahria's daughter could die and I wouldn't feel a thing.

I wasn't surprised when I woke up the next morning and Subashtian hadn't showed up. It was the reason I stayed up last night and came up with my final plan to get rid of Yahria. If this didn't work, I was packing up all my shit and getting out of dodge because I was sure it was going to get me killed. Esha didn't know it yet but once I got rid of Yahria she was next. All I wanted was my son to myself. Esha was unstable and any moment I felt that she would spill the beans on me.

"I'm assuming he didn't come home?" I asked Esha as she grabbed her purse to leave.

"No, he didn't and I called him several times to check on my son but he shut his phone off."

"He's probably with her."

"I mean, it's cool. I wish he would've said that because I could've been with Kesh last night instead of waiting up on him all night."

"Is that where you headed now?"

"No, I'm going to the mall to grab a few things and I'll be back."

As soon as she walked out of the door I went into Bash room and placed a bag of cocaine and weed in the bathroom drawer along with another one of my pregnancy tests. If this didn't get his attention, then I don't know what would. He had to bring his ass home first. Next stop was Yahria's apartment.

10

B ash

I LEFT E'shon with Yahria while I went to my house to let Esha know she had thirty days to get out because I was selling the house. My mind was made up and I was going to be with Yahria. Esha already knew it wasn't her. I just hoped that it wasn't any beef when I told her she needed to find her own place. When I arrived, no one was there. Taking this time, I started packing up shit but I started downstairs in my office. I hadn't been in here in so long that dust was collecting on everything. Wiping off my computer screen, I turned it on and waited for it to fire up.

I forgot all about my camera system that I had set up. Life was going pretty good, and I wasn't as paranoid as I was when Esha left me and E'shon. I was so afraid that someone was going to harm my son that I paid top dollar to get this installed. Double-clicking on the icon on the screen, the first thing that popped up was the last twenty-four hours. My mama and Esha was talking, I kept flipping through all the way until this morning. I zoomed in on my mama in my bathroom.

Her back was to the camera so I couldn't see what she was doing in there. The only time she ever went in my room was to get E'shon from me but other than that she never went in there. She definitely was up to no damn good. Now that I was interested in what the hell was going on in my house, I kept looking. There was no way to prepare my eyes for what I saw. Esha ass been fucking off and never intending on making shit work.

"Hey...I waited on you last night. Where is E'shon," Esha eased into the office.

This was not the same woman I fell in love with. From the first day I met her, she was very attentive even though she was an addict. It was like she was screaming for help. She pulled me in with her eyes. Now sitting here looking in her eyes, all I see is betrayal and I was using some of Yahria's techniques to try to keep myself calm. Yahria was really the only person that tried me by having people in my home. My mama tried it but that was shut down easily. Esha didn't have that privilege. She been letting a bitch stay all in my shit. Sleeping in my bed like they pay bills. Esha was starting to get uneasy because she went to scratching her arm.

"Who been in my house, Esha?"

"Nobody besides your mama."

"Let me rephrase the muthafuckin' question. Who you been fuckin' in my house?"

She swallowed hard before looking at me with tears in her eyes.

"Bash, you didn't want me so what was I supposed to do? I didn't mean for it to happen but it did. You left me stuck over here while you went to go be with your other baby mama. No matter how much I told you I was sorry, it was never enough," she cried.

"If you knew all that, why the fuck you in my house? Why the fuck you driving one of my cars and spending my damn money? I guess that's cool, huh? As the father of your child, I was trying to take care of you until you got on you damn feet. Get your shit," I raised up from the desk and grabbed her by her arm.

"You're hurting me, Bash."

"Go upstairs and get all your shit and get the fuck out."

"Why you so mad? Is it because you still want me but that girl blocking you from me?"

"Esha, I'll never want you again. You like a piece of damn trash to me right now. You got 'bout five minutes before I set this shit off in here. You didn't come with much but I'm being nice and letting you grab what you can in five minutes."

Esha rushed up the stairs as I stood there timing her. I never thought I would see this day coming but everyone that was connected to me except Yahria was starting to feel like leeches. The only way Yahria and I were going to make is if I released everyone that had a hold on me.

"Esha, you got ten seconds to get your ass down these steps and out the door. One...two...three...four."

Esha came running down the steps with one bag. She had clothes she was still stuffing in the bag as she ran down the steps, tripping and sliding down the last three. I was a gentleman, so I helped her up and made sure she wasn't hurt.

"Bash, I have something I need to tell you about your mama. She is the one-."

"What's going on in here?" my mama walked through the door.

"Nothing, I was just putting Esha out."

"Oh no you're not. She has nowhere else to go and you gave her this house if I'm correct."

"I did at first but I sold it so you need to get your shit out too."

"Sold it? Why would you do the mother of your child like that? I know I raised you better than that."

"I don't know if you did or not mama. Matter fact, you got five minutes to collect your shit too," I told my mama. "Now, Esha what was you saying 'bout my mama?" I turned my attention back to Esha.

"Umm...I was saying."

Esha had clammed up on me for some reason. Before my mama walked through the door she was ready to spill the beans on her and now that she was here she was nervous.

"It's nothing."

"Subashtian, you can't put her out."

"It's fine, Kelly. This is for the best. Like I told you before, all I want is Bash to be happy and she makes him happy."

I caught the evil eye my mama gave Esha but I brushed it off.

"Ma, go get some of your stuff."

"I'll come back and get it. You putting the poor girl out without nothing, at least let me give her a ride to where she's going."

"I don't give a damn what y'all do. I need your stuff out of here within the next three days," I told her as they walked out the door.

MY HOUSE WAS in the process of closing on the deal, and I was still cooped up in my condo with my son. I tried talking to Yahria but for some reason she was acting funny with me. She wouldn't even let me come over to her apartment to spend time with her and my daughter. She would drop Kai off and leave. She promised to have dinner with me tonight so we hired Farah for the night so we could see where we were going with our relationship.

Since my condo was bigger, Yahria brought Kai over there and Farah watched them at my place. Yahria was sitting in the passenger side of my car smelling and looking good. Her thighs were out in her short ass purple dress. She bobbed her head to the YFN Lucci that was playing through the speakers. She was wearing the ring I made for her but it wasn't on the finger I wanted it on. She had it on the opposite hand.

"Why you not wearing your ring correctly?" I asked her. She raised her hand and the diamond glistened from the street lights we passed.

"What's wrong with this hand? I don't want nobody to think I'm engaged or married 'cause I'm not."

"You know what hand it supposed to be on though."

"Of course, I know that but I thought it was a gift for my birthday.

I thought I could wear it how I wanted too until my husband came and put something on the other hand."

"Yahria, don't be funny 'cause I'm not in the mood."

"Shit, I ain't either."

I pulled the car over so we could talk because obviously she had something on her chest.

"What's the issue? Why you been acting funny the last three weeks? I've been trying to spend time with you but you pushing me away again. What's up with that?"

Yahria looked at me and back out of the window. I hated when she shut down on me. It was hard to get her to talk when she was too pissed off or she didn't want to deal with it. That was a barrier I hadn't broke, with her yet.

"You gon' talk to me or we gon' go to dinner and just eat and not talk?"

"I'm 'bout whatever you 'bout, Bash."

"So if I wanted to fuck you for a few hours you down with that too?"

Nope!"

"Then you ain't bout what I'm 'bout then. Tell me what got you so pissed off with me?"

"Did you fuck Esha, Bash? If you lie to me then I'll cut you off just like I did when I found out Pharaoh was fuckin' your mama." She covered her mouth as soon as she said it.

"Fuck you just say?"

"Nothing, don't worry 'bout it."

"Yahria, repeat what the fuck you just said."

"Bash, I didn't mean for it to come out that way. It's just I've been under a lot of stress with this relationship. Somebody came to me with proof that Esha was pregnant from you again and it hurt so I avoided you."

The fact she just laid on me that my mama was fucking Pharaoh had just gone out the window when she revealed to me what was bothering her.

"You can't come to your man 'bout shit like that? I thought we were better than that. I don't give a fuck what my mama doing with that nigga. My only focus is working on me and you. Shit, if he fucks her right, she'll stay out my business. Now where you get this information from?"

"You still haven't answered my question, Bash."

"What was the question?"

"Did you fuck Esha?"

"Hell no!"

"Yea, a'ight. You've been known to lie so I don't know what to believe."

"Girl, I ain't lied to your lil' ass yet. You not 'bout to fuck up my night with this bullshit though. You can believe what you want to believe. I should have fucked her since you ain't giving it up."

Yahria reached over and slapped me in my mouth, drawing blood. This was her last time putting her hands on me and I not react. I put the car in drive and busted a U-turn in the middle of the streets almost costing us our life. We hadn't got far from my condo but I was taking her ass home. If she wanted to act crazy she could do that shit on her own without me being a part of her life. It took me about five minutes to pull up to her gate and punch her code in so we could get in.

"Get the fuck outta my car, Yahria."

"I'm not doing shit until you take me to get my daughter and my car."

"Yahria, this my last time asking you nicely to get the fuck up outta of my shit."

"Or what? What you gon' do Bash? Not a damn thing just like you ain't did shit this whole relationship with your mama. I asked you a simple question and you come back with a smart as remark like you should have fucked her. How you expect me to act? But let me go jump on Pharaoh dick and you want to jack me up. Better yet, let me go do that just to show you and your mama, I'm not the bitch to fuck with."

Yahria snatched my door open and slammed it shut. By the time I whipped my car into a parking spot she had disappeared in her building. I had a spare key to her apartment; I just never used it out of respect. I made it up to the doorman but he wouldn't let me in.

"Nigga, let me the fuck in," I told him.

"She told me not to let you in. I'm sorry, I'm just doing my job, sir."

I walked away to my car and came back and tapped on the door with the butt of my nine millimeter.

"Open this bitch before I shoot your damn hands off and then you won't be able to push any buttons for the rest of your life," I threatened.

His eyes got big as saucers as he pressed the button to let me in. I took the elevator up to Yahria's floor. I was going to play nice and see if she would open the door for me so I knocked and rang the doorbell.

"Yahria, open the door so we can talk," I calmly said.

"Bash, get away from my damn door. Don't bring your ass back over here until you bring me my child," she said from the other side of the door.

"Yahria, I'm being nice so could you open the door. I got a key so you might as well open it."

From the other side of the door I could hear her putting the chain on the door. Now she was starting to piss me off.

"That still can't keep me out. I'm only giving you a few seconds to open the door or I'm coming in and it ain't gone be by key," I said cocking my gun and aiming it at the door.

The sound of the chains being removed and door unlocking was music to my ears. Yahria stood to the door with her hand in her hip. The fact that I was pointing a gun at her didn't even faze her.

"Put the damn gun away before my neighbors call the cops. What the hell you want?"

"You getting ready to go fuck your ex-nigga?"

"Bash, I'm tired and I don't have the energy to argue with you. If you don't want to know the answer to that then don't ask questions."

"Oh, I want to know the answer so I can know if I need to beat your lil' ass or not."

"Beat who ass? You know better than that right? You or your gun don't scare me. Why you worried 'bout what I'm finna do? I didn't bother you while you was fucking Esha."

"I ain't fuck that girl. Shit, I been trying to sleep with you for almost a month now and you got me thinking somebody else getting it."

"Hmph," Yahria huffed before I slammed her back into the wall.

"Y'all wearing the nice Bash thin and I'm getting tired of playing with y'all. What the fuck does *hmph* mean?"

"If you don't want your lip bigger than what it is you better release me," Yahria warned.

A knock at her door distracted us just enough for Yahria to slip out of my grip.

"Who the hell is that?"

Yahria didn't answer. She went to the door and opened it. The heat that was building in my body was rising quickly as soon as he opened his mouth.

"Hey, the doorman called me and told me you may need some help. Everything cool?"

"Let that pussy nigga in here. I'm tired of his ass too," I said loud enough for him to hear me.

"No, y'all not 'bout to tear up my shit and get me put out."

"Watch out, Yahria. What the fuck you say to me pretty boy ass nigga."

We stood toe to toe. This nigga had a little heart and I respected that. But only one of us was going to walk out this bitch and it was gone be me.

"Why the fuck you keep popping the fuck up when me and my girl trying to work shit out? What you ride the neighborhood or some shit 'cause I know you can't afford to stay on this side of town."

"Oh, she your girl again? I could've sworn she was free game. Shit, we was just together trying to see if we could pick back up where we left off."

The smirk he had on his face set me off and all I saw was red. My fist connected with jaw making saliva spew from his mouth. He was dazed from the first blow and I had no intentions of slowing up. That was the benefit of me working out and staying in shape. My stamina was like none other. While he was still trying to figure out what day of the week it was, I had done hit him three more times, knocking him out cold.

"I never thought you were a hoe until tonight. You ain't got to worry 'bout me fuckin' with your ass no more. Take your raggedy ass back where the fuck you came from. You'll never be shit with your rat ass," I told Yahria.

She quickly picked up a vase and hurled it at my head but I ducked just in time.

"I'll be all that, you dumb bitch. I don't want neither one of y'all niggas. He got your mama pregnant and you fuckin' crack head ass bitches. I regret the day I even opened my legs for you and I wish I would've swallowed Kai so I wouldn't have to deal with your uppity ass. Get your ass out my shit."

"I'll have Farah bring Kai home. Find you another way 'round 'cause the car staying with me."

"Bitch ass nigga! You a whole hoe for that shit but it's cool. You can take this too," she pulled the ring off and hit me in my face.

"Don't get mad when you see another woman wearing your shit."

"Bash, I don't give a fuck. Go get your life nigga and let me live mine."

The man I once was, was no longer. This love shit had turned me into my old self and I was ready to kill anybody in my damn way at this point. Everybody except my kids could kiss my muthafuckin' ass.

ah-Yah

"Y'ALL NEED TO fix this shit, 'cause I can't deal with your damn attitude," Neca said as she cut my hair off.

"Neca, I'm not fixing shit that I didn't mess up. I didn't tell my doorman to call Pharaoh ass; he just popped the fuck up out of nowhere. I'm used to fussing with Bash. He never puts his hands on me; all he do is talk shit and then try to sleep with me."

"But didn't I tell you it was another side of that nigga that you didn't want to see? Now, look at you sitting here cutting all your damn hair off. Your titties swollen 'cause he won't bring Kai home to nurse. You really done seen what it's like to be fuckin' with a real boss. Now you got to go over there to see your child."

"He just doing that shit 'cause he want to see me but ain't got the balls enough to say he miss me."

"Guh, I don't know. He was just with some bitch from 'round the way in the club the other night and when I checked him 'bout it, he said you told him to live his life."

All the blood drained out of my face when Neca told me that. Bash wasn't even the type of man to go fuck with some random chick. I don't even know who this man was that Neca was speaking on. Bash was better than that. We hadn't talked since the incident and it's been about a month. He dropped Kai off twice since then but most of the time she's over there and he wants me to come there to spend time with her and E'shon. It didn't bother me 'cause he wasn't allowed back at my place unless he was dropping the kids off and he was only allowed to stay downstairs.

"Who was the chick?" I asked Neca.

"Bitch, I'm not 'bout to tell you who it was for you to go running up in that girl face. Don't forget I know the old you."

"I just want to know who can clearly disrespect the fact that me and Bash still gon' fuck with each other regardless."

"Sus, Bash free game right now. He be in the club more than the damn DJ."

"So, instead of him bringing me my baby, he leaves her home with Farah and go stick his dick in whoever will show him some attention?"

"Pretty much."

"Why you just now telling me this?" I turned around to look at her.

"'Cause you know how I feel 'bout niggas. If he doing him, you need to do you. All you do is fuckin' work and take your ass in the house, waiting for him to beg you back like he always do. This time sus, he may not be coming back. Now that's truth for your ass. Don't get me wrong, I love y'all ass together and I want it to work but you can't put your damn life on pause for a nigga."

"You right and that's why I'm taking my ass out tonight. I got this new piece I want to wear since I done grew a lil' ass and titties."

"Nah! Hell nah! We are not going to a club that he frequents. A bitch ain't got time to be beatin' up on hoes and they pulling at my damn weave."

"I'm not worried 'bout Bash. We got over seven clubs here. Pick one and let's go, shit. I ain't been out in so long, it's overdue."

"We gon' go but the first time I think some trouble coming our way, we out that bitch. You got too much to lose and none of these hoes worth it. As long as you know where Bash heart at, no need to fight with a temporary bitch. Let that man get his nuts off and when he realizes that's all these hoes gon' ever be, he'll be back begging. At least that's what I'm hoping for."

"It don't matter either way. It has been peaceful with him and Pharaoh out of my life. Maybe I should try dating again too. I did jump from Pharaoh to him and then ended up pregnant. I don't know what it's like to date different guys."

"Good luck with that," Neca stated as she sponged my curls on my short hair.

"What does that mean?"

"See, men like Bash can dish it but can't take it. That's why his rage was so bad when Pharaoh popped up at your spot. Y'all ain't been together since the reveal party and Kai is almost three months. Don't you find it strange he don't want you with nobody else but him. No doubt he loves you but if you gon' date it damn sure better be a nigga from out of town."

"Fuck my life," I sighed.

"This cut looks good on your lil' head ass. I can't wait to see you dress this shit up."

I ran my fingers over my now bald head. It was just enough hair there to form some small curls and she dyed it blondish pink. It was really dope and I was feeling it. Everyone knew that I was stylish and the outfit I was wearing tonight was going to set this right off.

"Bitch, I'll meet you at the club 'cause you tend to get with a nigga and forget I'm there," I told Neca, as I gathered my things.

"I always have an eye on you though."

"Yea, I bet you do. I'll see you tonight."

Since Bash called himself taking my car from me, I went and bought a Lexus with my hard earned cash. When he saw me pull up to his condo in it, he was salty as fuck but I didn't care at all. My car was sitting in the same spot I left it in the night he beat Pharaoh ass. Bash wanted me to beg him to give me my car back but he didn't really know me well. I would've caught the damn bus before I begged a nigga for anything. I didn't ask for the car, so I damn sure wasn't about to ask for it back.

Farah texted me to bring some milk over because Kai was out. Since Bash was being a crazy, possessive nigga and trying to keep our child hostage to get back at me, I was pumping milk and freezing it to keep my breast from hurting. I sent her a text back asking if Bash was home. I wanted to feed her off my breast to relieve some of the pressure. I headed in her direction when she told me he was gone to work.

Farah opened the door with Kai in her arms. I grabbed my baby and kissed her before she started trying to scoot down to my breast. I sat on the sofa next to E'shon who was playing on his tablet. Letting Kai latch on, I turned my attention to Farah who was standing there staring at me.

"What Farah?"

"Y'all still playing this tit for tat game?"

"I'm not playing any games, Farah. I'm doing the same shit I was doing when Bash and I was talking every day. I work and go home."

"He miss you."

"No he doesn't. He's partying and having a good time with different women. If that's what he believes missing me is, I don't want it."

"He's slipping but there haven't been any women coming up here. He takes good care of these kids and he still talks about you."

"I'll pass. Bash is possessive as hell. What kind of man keep his newborn from their mama?"

"The type of man that knows that's the only way he'll be able to lay eyes on the woman he loves. He knows damn well if you get Kai, you'll keep her away from him and he won't see either of y'all."

"It's still selfish no matter which way you put it."

"It may be but what do you expect when a woman like Kelly raised him."

"Tuh, you got a point."

I burped Kai and put her to sleep before I left to go home and grab her some more milk. Bash was getting out of his car when I pulled back up. To avoid seeing him, I asked Farah to come downstairs and get the milk when Bash walked in the house. It ain't like he saw me pull up anyway because he was too busy caking a bitch on the phone.

I LET the music from my speakers get me in the mood as I finished getting dressed. For a moment, I changed my mind about going to the club but heard about a party that was going to be popping because Blac Youngsta was coming through. I was trying to make all connections for my business. Standing in my mirror, I practiced my twerk since it's been a minute. Kai gave me something to actually shake now. Somebody son was about to be in trouble tonight. My cat was freshly waxed and I was smelling divine.

The outfit I made was a two piece but towards the end of making it, I sewed the sides together to give it a one-piece effect. My stomach was out and the back dipped low and stopped right before my crack was exposed. Everything was hugging me and the bottom of the pants flared out just a little. The bright floral colors made my hair look even better than it did earlier today. I had no makeup, just lash extensions and gloss.

Neca was already waiting on me when I arrived. I let valet park my car because there was no way I was about to park a block away and walk back with heels on. The line was long but Neca and I decided to spend a little money so we could get our own section. It felt good to finally be able to go half or get the tab for my best friend. For years, she made sure I was straight. Security walked us to our section and closed the rope on us.

"What you want to drink?" I asked Neca, as she checked out the scene.

"You know I'll drink anything."

I ordered us a few bottles as we got into the groove of the music. Neca had invited a few niggas in our section but not before charging their ass. We split the money and pocketed it. They were from out of town so it was cool that none of us knew each other. They added more bottles to the section and we vibed a few hours until Blak got up there to perform. He had the club so lit that hoes were popping pussy on the stage just to get took back to the room with him. All I wanted to do was slide him my card so I could style him one time.

"Now I may be just a lil' tipsy but ain't that Bash and his homeboy over there?" Neca whispered in my ear.

"Yea, that's him. As long he stays on his side and don't get disrespectful, I'm good."

"You sure? We can go to another club."

"Bitch, all the money I paid to get in here. I'm not leaving, plus Blac got this bitch live so hell to tha no I'm not leaving. He got a chick keeping him occupied so we good," I told her.

"Bash couldn't do no better than that? That hoe weave nappy as fuck on the ends."

"Leave her Yaki hair alone now. Everybody can't afford that shit you wear in your head."

We both laughed as the music changed. I had been wilding all night and as bad as I wanted to put on a show for Bash, I couldn't. Blac came over the mic and asked for two bad females to join him up on stage for his song *Booty*. The light went to shining all over the club and landed on Neca and I. I backed up so no one would see me but Neca grabbed my arm and snatched me out the section towards the stage.

"Girl, hell nah. I'm not 'bout to go up there."

"You know damn well your ass be dancing to this song. You ain't got to do what these hoes doing but we need to get him to take your business card. Now get your ass up here and be cute if you got to," Neca pulled me up the stairs.

The beat dropped and the girls on the stage went to popping their ass to the beat of the music. A few months ago that would've been me. I don't know what made me look at Bash. We locked eyes while the nappy head hoe kissed all over his neck while he watched to see what I was going to do. I always told myself that if I didn't make it out the hood, I was going to be a stripper but I was too skinny. Now that my skinny days were over and Bash was on some other shit, why not shake my ass.

The chorus hit...*girl I wanna see you, twerk. I'll throw a lil' money if you twerk.* That was all I need to make this ass bounce. The crowd went crazy and cash was flying in the air. Neca was standing there gassing me up and grabbing the money. By the time the song was over, I had made all my money back that I spent to come in here and I got to talk to Blac behind the scene and give him my card.

"Bitch, we got to go after that performance. Bash gone show the hell out," Neca said heading back to our section.

"Yea, I'm 'bout to go anyway. I'm just gon' grab my shit and get out of dodge."

We grabbed our stuff that the dudes were watching and slipped out of the club before any shit popped off. I checked to see if Bash was still in his section before we walked out and the only person there was the chick he was hugged up with. I was glad I made it out without having to fight my way out. Making sure I drove the speed limit, I checked my mirrors a few times to make sure I wasn't being followed.

I parked my car in my spot and got out of my car. I had my shoes in my hand and my key card ready to enter my building when Bash ass appeared out of the dark. Something told me to take my ass to Neca house or Big Ma house. He was mad as hell because his face was balled up and his eyes were red.

"Bash, please not right now," I pleaded.

"You showing your ass in the club now? You got everybody looking at me and shit."

"Can I go in my building please? You drunk and I don't want to argue with you."

"No, you gon' stand your fuckin' ass right here and answer my damn question."

"What is your question, Bash?" I crossed my arms, waiting on his drunk ass to get his words out.

"Why you embarrassing me?"

"Bash, I did not embarrass you. Obviously, everyone knows I'm not your girl anymore. I don't drive the same car and you were hugged up with a woman tonight. I'm assuming that's who put them makeup stains on your shirt."

He looked down to see what I was talking about and looked back at me. I wanted to go inside but I had to walk past him to even get to the door and I didn't want him touching me. Turning my back, I started walking back to my car but he grabbed me as I reached for the door.

"You could've been came and got that damn car back. I've told you over and over again when it comes to you, it's yours."

"Bash, you are drunk and we don't need to be around each other 'cause it's always some bullshit. If I get in trouble with your ass out here again, I'm getting put out."

"Good, then you can bring your ass where you supposed to be at?"

"And where is that?"

"Home, muthafucka! Where your children at."

"Bash, back up please." I tried to push him off of me but he was pressing all his weight on me making my back hurt on my door handle.

"You don't like this Bash do you? Y'all kept poking the damn bear until this is what you get. You don't like the nice guy."

"No, your mama them poked the bear but you taking it out on me. I haven't done shit to you, ever! If you want to be a fuckin' drunk, then bring me the kids and I'll take care of them. Now, get the fuck out of my face."

Bash grabbed my face and kissed me. The taste of Hennessey was evident all over his tongue. I missed the hell out of him so I invited his kiss until I thought about that bitch he was just with a few hours ago.

"Get the fuck off me," I said, being able to push him off this time.

"What the fuck you want from me, Yahria? Huh? I can't even damn function without your lil' ass. I got our daughter thinking your ass would come beg to get her so I could beg you to take me back but you didn't. I take your car thinking you would come and get it and you didn't. I've run out of shit to do, Yahria."

"Why you want to be with a rat ass bitch, Bash? Huh? Ain't that what you called me when you beat Pharaoh ass? You said a lot of disrespectful shit that night. You don't think that shit hurt me? Well, you're wrong. When you love someone, you don't call them out their name."

"So, it's cool to put your hands on me then?"

I forgot I had busted his lip that night which is why he showed out in the first place. We were unstable as fuck but there was no doubt that when we were together, we were unstoppable. Bash came back towards me but this time he was softer. He ran his hand down my face causing shivers to run down my spine. So many nights I wanted to call Bash and tell him that I wanted him but every time I tried, something stopped me.

"Yahria, I know you tired of me begging you and if you tell me no this last time I promise I won't bother you anymore for real this time. I'll let Kai come home and I'll see her on your terms. You did something to me and I can't figure out how to move on without you. Seeing folks throw money at you while you was shaking your ass on stage pissed me off and I felt like it was my fault you was up there behaving like that."

"Did you sleep with any of those girls people been seeing you with? Please, don't lie 'bout it 'cause I don't want to be with you and then nine months down the line a baby pop up."

"I can promise you I never slept with any of them. If I wouldn't have seen you tonight though, I would have slept with ol' girl."

"Really? The one with the bad weave that was kissing on you?"

"Hell yea, she was ready to do it all just to be with me."

"You sound ridiculous. She was willing to do all the things I was already doing except bringing someone else in our bedroom."

"Shit, how long you expected me to have blue balls? I'm sure you planned on sleeping with one of them niggas that was in your section."

"Never that. If I sleep with someone it was going to be someone I was familiar with. I don't do random one night stands."

"Let's do one now then. 'Cause I don't really know your ass like that and you don't know me."

"Give me your phone," I told him, holding my hand out.

"For what?"

"If you want me then you need to delete all them hoes out your phone."

"Ain't nobody in there."

"Let me see that for myself."

Bash reached in his pocket and gave it to me. I scrolled through and saw a few text messages between him and the chick from tonight. I blocked her number and any other number I didn't know.

"Now you need to do that shit to yours too."

"I ain't got nothing in my phone."

"So, that nigga ain't in your phone no more."

"Nope!"

"Your pussy ass doorman at work tonight?" Bash asked.

"No, it's another dude here tonight."

"Let's go upstairs so we can ride this stress out of each other."

I grabbed Bash hand and walked him in my building. As soon as the elevator closed, Bash was peeling my clothes off of me. The sexual tension was so high that tonight was going to be one for the books. Thank goodness I took my birth control pill today because we were about to go a few rounds.

12

Pharaoh

I DON'T KNOW what the hell was wrong with me. I guess when you can't have the one you want you go to the one that wants you. Now I was feeling like a complete fool with this lunatic ass bitch, Kelly. She was big and pregnant but that didn't stop her ass from doing something crazy every day. She was losing her mind because she had no idea where Bash moved and she couldn't keep tabs on the nigga no more. She stalked Yahria page all day until her phone goes dead. The only conclusion she could come up with is they were back together while my baby mama got a relationship with his baby mama. This whole situation was some shit off of television. It was partially my fault because Yahria would still be with me if it wasn't for Kesh.

"Are you going to lay your ass 'round all day today too or you gon' get up and do something to your hair?" I asked Kelly.

"I have an appointment today so I'll be getting up."

Her old ass went to the doctor every week because she was too old to be carrying a baby in the first place. A piece of me was hoping and wishing the baby wouldn't make it. It was selfish but Kelly thought she owned me because she was pregnant from me and even that was still up in the air. She was talking to this old ass white man a few weeks ago and she didn't know that I knew she was telling him it was his baby. Now I knew where the new car came from. He was paying her ass to be quiet. Only reason I was here was to keep an eye on her ass because she was unstable.

She would kill me if she knew I was starting a fresh relationship with a girl on the other side of town. Protecting her was my first priority and that was why I was still over here with Kelly every night laying under her like we were so in love. I hadn't touched her in so long that I don't even think she remembers.

Brushing my teeth and washing my face, I put my clothes back on that I wore yesterday so I could go home and get fresh. I was taking my girl out today because she had been so patient with this situation. I was trying to find the perfect time to tell Kelly that we were done for real. Shit, to me we been done. We hadn't slept together; it was like we were roommates. Kelly was the type of bitch you had to break up with her in public or she would kill you.

"What time you coming back?" Kelly asked without moving out of her spot.

"It will be late. If it's too late I'll just go back to my spot."

"No, you need to bring your ass back here. I don't give a damn how late it is."

"Yes massa," I said grabbing my shit and walking out.

Taelor was everything I was looking for. Since being with Yah-Yah for so long, it was hard for someone to match her loyalty. Taelor had the spunk I needed but was sweet and conducted herself as a woman as well. She was something like Yah-Yah is now. She didn't let me run over her but she still let me be her man. She had a three year old son that I met. She met my daughters as well and now we were trying to see how far this thing goes.

I talked with Taelor about all the shit Yah-Yah and I went through and now the battle I was going through with Kelly. She understood that I was trying to protect her and her son. Taelor lived at least forty minutes away from the city in a nice quiet neighborhood. She worked a regular job as an office manager at a plastic surgery center and made pretty decent money. I like the fact that she knew what I did but she never held her hand out wanting anything from me. I always made sure she was straight, without her asking.

Taelor was checking the mail when I pulled up behind her car. Her smile brightened my day as I got out and greeted her with a kiss and smack on the ass. Today was her day and we were doing anything she wanted. Her son was out of town with his father so it was just us today and after we got done I planned on spending my night between her thighs and showing her just how much I appreciated her.

"You looking good in this outfit," I told her as she spun around.

"I was afraid you wouldn't like it because I'm showing all my goodies."

"Niggas know you belong to me."

She was wearing one of those two-piece things with all her stomach out and the pants were tight as hell on her big ass. She was still cute though. She had her little toes polished pink and her slides matched her outfit.

"Yah-Yah posted some pieces on her IG page and I bought a few. I hope you don't mind."

"What? Nah...nah, I don't mind."

Since me and Bash's fight, I called myself letting Yah-Yah go. I hadn't seen her or talk to her which was a good thing. The only time I would get a glimpse is if Kelly was stalking her and I was looking but other than that, I avoid any area she was going to be in. It took me a good minute to get her out of my system.

"Let me grab my purse and I'll be ready."

I opened the door for Taelor and waited for her to put her seat-belt on before I walked around to get in the driver seat. My past relationship taught me how to be a better man and father, especially since I had girls. I let my sunroof back so we could enjoy the nice breeze as we made our way to the carnival that was being held at the beach.

I was a nigga from the hood so going to the carnival and getting on rides was something I wasn't used to but Tae had me doing things I never done before. We got on a few rides and played a few games so I could win her some ugly ass stuffed animals. We were grown, acting like teenagers but it felt good. Tae told me she was hungry so I let her rest while I went to grab something to eat and drink. I didn't expect to see Yah-Yah standing there talking to her when I returned.

"Hey, I was just telling her about you and how great you are."

Yah-Yah smiled as she shifted her daughter to the other arm. I sat the food down and didn't say anything.

"I'm sure he's a good man to you. It was nice meeting you face to face and let me know if you need any clothes made. Pharaoh has plenty of money to spend," Yah-Yah stated.

"I hit you up in your DM if I think of anything," Tae told her.

Instead of them ending their conversation, Tae started talking about the baby which led Yah-Yah into talking about breastfeeding and shit. A part of me wanted to interrupt they ass but I was enjoying my view of Yah-Yah's ass. I thought I was over her ass until the scent of her was around me.

"Tae, your food getting cold and I ain't going to get anymore," I told her.

"I got to get back to Bash anyway. It was good talking to you. Good seeing you too Pharaoh."

I nodded at her as she left. Tae nudged me as I watched until she was out of my sight.

"She's beautiful. I see why you so stuck on her."

"I'm not stuck on her. It's all 'bout you baby."

"I hope so."

Tae kisses me and enjoyed her food as I stared off into the crowded people hoping to see Yah-Yah one more time. The sun was starting to set, and I was ready to go home and take a bath. We got back to Tae's place, and she went and ran us a bath while I slipped out of my clothes. She lit some candles and turned on some music. It didn't take a lot to please her and she took care of me like I was a king. There was definitely a future between us and I couldn't wait to give her the world.

~

Looking over at Tae, I grabbed my ringing phone to shut it off. The only person that could be calling was Kelly crazy ass. The time read twelve minutes after three in the morning. I didn't even remember falling asleep. Since it was so late, there was no need to leave now. Raising up out the bed, I walked to the bathroom with my dick swinging to go take a piss.

The light flicked off and the door closed. Tae loved to prank but I was too tired for that shit right now. I reached for the light and turned it on to see blood on my hand.

"What the fuck?" I looked at myself in the mirror. I had small splatters of blood on my face and chest but I had no cuts.

"You ever heard that you need to be careful who you lay down with?"

"Kelly, what the fuck have you done?"

"You didn't come home and you wouldn't answer your phone so I came over to make sure I won't have this problem anymore."

"How the fuck you knew where I was?"

"Location on your phone," she grinned.

I launched at her and we fell in the tub, knocking the shower curtain down making it hit me in the head. Instead of me being on top of Kelly she was now on top of me with her gun cocked and ready to blow my damn head off. She was on some fatal attraction shit and I only hoped Tae was still breathing when this shit was over.

"Now you gon' get your ass up out the tub and help me wrap her body up."

"I ain't doing shit," I said before she hit me in the head with her gun.

"You do what the fuck I tell you to do or take your ass to jail. I got this scene set up to where you can take the fall for it or a complete stranger can. Which one you want?"

We stared at each other with a brief pause.

"That's What the fuck I thought."

With all that stomach in front of her, you would think she was tired and weak but she yanked me out the tub and pushed me back towards the bedroom. The tears filled my eyes seeing Tae lying there stabbed and sliced up. How the hell did I not hear or feel anything? I could've saved her.

"And before your punk ass start trying to plot, I got one police friend on speed dial now focus 'cause we only have a limited amount of time in order for this to work."

The tears fell as Tae's body hit the floor with a thud as Kelly pulled her from the bed. She showed me what she was really capable of and the shit had me shook.

"Stop fuckin' standing there and help so I won't go into labor. I'm already contracting too early as is."

"You shouldn't be your ass here and you wouldn't be hurting."

"Maybe if you would have came home then I wouldn't be now would I? You thought you were going to have a relationship without me knowing it didn't you? I wanted to kill the bitch and her son but I knew you were going to slip up. Now here we are, wrapping this hoe up."

"You crazy as hell."

"I know! My dead husband couldn't stand my jealous rages, thankfully I never caught him cheating like I did you."

Carrying Tae's body through the house and into her car was sickening. Knowing her son would never have his mama again bothered the hell out of me. Some kind of way, Kelly had to pay for this shit. As the sky went from black to a light orange, we dumped Tae's body in a wooded area that I had never seen. What I did notice was a bunch of red flags sticking out of the ground. Out of my side view, Kelly stuck one in the ground next to Tae's body.

"What are the flags for?"

"Bodies. Now bring your ass on because my water just broke."

"Kelly you are not even far enough to be having the baby."

Taking a quick look, I counted at least twelve. Once her ass got attached to all them machines, I was getting the fuck away from her before she got me jammed up.

elly

"So, you're saying you caught him cheating on you with the other woman and you told him he had to choose. He left the house and returned a few hours later upset with you which sent you in labor?" The detective asked, making sure he was giving me his undivided attention.

"Yes," I wiped the fake tears from my face.

"Taelor Wells has been reported missing for two days. Her ex-husband went to drop their child off and she wasn't there. Do you think Mr. Pharaoh would harm her?"

"He's been known to put his hands on me when he gets upset so I'm pretty sure he did something to her."

"We'll make sure to keep you updated. Please make sure you call us if he contacts you and I'm sorry for your loss."

"Thank you," I stated.

As soon as he closed the door, I hopped out of the bed to grab my phone out of my purse. I had an important phone call to make that couldn't wait. Dialing the number, I climbed back in bed and waited for an answer.

"Hello?"

"I need a favor."

"No, my last man died so the answer is no!"

"Listen, I'm paying well."

"I'm listening."

"I need you to find somebody and bring them to me alive. Don't send one of your guys because we both know how the last one ended up. I want you to do it."

"I'll meet you tomorrow so we can discuss it," he said before hanging up.

The doctor had already made rounds and I was scheduled to go home on tomorrow. I told them to cremate the ugly ass baby and give me the ashes. I knew once he came out who the baby belonged to and Pharaoh was definitely not the father. The loss didn't bother me because I had no business being pregnant in the first place. I only did it to keep Pharaoh. Not that I loved him, I didn't want no one else to have him and his dick was to die for.

I heard a tap on my door and the door popped open. I wasn't expecting any company and no one knew I was here so I was waiting on them to reveal themselves from around the privacy curtain. I'm not sure why my emotions got the best of me but to see Subashtian standing there with roses and a teddy bear brought tears to my eyes.

"I know we ain't fuckin' with each other like that but you still my mama and I was concerned."

He stood there as handsome as the day I had him. I don't think I would've been so evil if it was just the two of us like it once was.

"Thank you for checking on me. I had a feeling I wasn't going to be able to carry full term. You know your mama ain't no spring chicken anymore."

"Awww, you still got it," he laughed.

"How's E'shon?"

"He's getting big. Yahria finally got him potty trained and he's able to say his alphabets."

"That boy should be with his mama."

"As far as I'm concerned, he is with his mama. Yahria helped raise him. Besides, Esha enjoying her life with that chick. I don't want to disturb that."

"I'm sorry you had to find out that way. How often do you look at those tapes?" I asked, trying to make sure he hadn't seen anything else.

"I got rid of them. There was no need for them anymore and I don't need a security system at my condo because it's just us and I'm not paranoid anymore."

"That's good to know."

"So, where your nigga at? He gone to grab you something to eat?"

"No, it's just me," I sadly said.

"Damn, my bad. I didn't know."

"It's cool. I go home tomorrow so I'll be fine."

"You sure you need to be home by yourself? I got an extra bedroom if you need for a few weeks until the doctor clears you."

"Yahria hates me and I don't want to invade her space."

"Me and Yahria in a good place now. I'm sure she'll understand."

"I'll see, son."

"I insist. Just until you heal."

"Okay, if you say so."

"We're never there. She works most of the day and so do I do. You'll be there with Farah and the kids."

"Thank you, Subashtian."

"No problem. I'll be back to get you tomorrow."

When he left, I pulled my small notebook out of my purse and crossed out Taelor's name. I had three more names in the list and sadly, Pharaoh was one of them.

14

Yah-Yah

MY NERVES WERE GETTING the best of me as I waited for my mama to walk through the door. I begged Neca to take me to get a Xanax but she refused. My leg tapped against the steel table as I watched everyone around me talk with their mothers, aunties and grandmothers. Sitting in here really made me grateful for all those times Bash fought for me to get out. The only way I end up back in here is if a bitch threatens my child.

I looked around nervously as I rubbed my hands together. The wait was starting to take a toll on me, it had been at least fifteen minutes and she still hadn't appeared. Maybe she didn't want to see me. It took me some time to make my mind up if I wanted to come or not, so she probably changed her mind by now.

"My mama told me how beautiful you grew up to be but I never thought you would be this damn fine."

I turned around to see my mama standing behind me looking like she hadn't aged since the last time I seen her. My emotions were mixed and I didn't know if I should hug her or go in on her with all the questions I had. She pulled me up from the bench and in for a hug. It was awkward at first until I decided to hug her back. We sat down and stared at each other for the longest before she spoke.

"I'm open to take anything you got to say. I'm just glad you're here."

"I had all these things I wanted to say but now that I'm here and I see you, I'm speechless."

"I'll start with the questions then. How have you been? Mama told me you got kids and a possible husband," she nudged me and smiled. "I also heard 'bout a bitch that been giving you grief. Who is it?"

"First off, Big Ma talk too damn much. I had one child which is a little girl I name Kai Rose."

"Rose? Like after me?"

"Yes. The other child is my boyfriend's son; he's about to be two but I've been with him since he was a baby so he's starting to call me mama."

"And this bitch?"

"It's my boyfriend mama. It's like she hates me and we don't even know each other. I believe she has an infatuation with her son or some shit. It's a lot to the story and it would take the whole visit to tell you all the drama in my life."

"I had a few run-ins with my mother in law, too, especially once her sorry ass son knocked me up and disappeared."

"I'm glad you spoke on that. Who is my damn daddy?"

"Girl, you don't even want to know him. He's a bum now but back in the day I thought he was going to be the biggest boss of the city."

"Who?"

"You know the man that Big Ma feeds and let shower twice a week?"

I went through my memory bank trying to remember. As a teenager, I did see a man early in the morning coming out of the bathroom. Big Ma always tried to make it seem like she got up early because she couldn't sleep but it was to have food ready for him before I got up.

"You kidding, right?"

"Nope! He got a hold of some bad dope and had a nervous breakdown. He went from balling and flaunting hoes in my face to being dead broke and homeless. He still homeless and to be honest I still love him. I tried my best to help him but his mind was like a sixteen-year-old boy."

"What's his name?"

"Tony but everyone called him Ton back in the day. He was the sweetest person but I don't think he was ready for kids. He told me he wasn't financially stable to care for me and a child. My heart couldn't take getting rid of you and I told him that so he left. The whole time I was pregnant with you, I cried because my heart had been broken. Occasionally, he would pop up just to sleep with me but never anything else."

"Like why did you hide it from me for so long?"

"By the time you were old enough, I was in the streets so heavy and your daddy was roaming 'round with his head in the clouds. I was already an embarrassment to you why make it worse telling you your daddy is a looney toon."

"I never gave a damn what people thought 'bout me. It was important to know that my daddy has been right up under my nose all this time and you or Big Ma never said nothing."

"I begged my mama not to tell you. She only did what I asked her to do."

"Why the streets, ma?"

"Mama was on a fixed income and someone had to pay the bills. I wasn't there all the time but I kept the lights on and the water running for you. Money and credit cards were my love. I was on my last strike and here I am. I'm just glad you didn't turn out like me."

"Big Ma did what she could."

"Will I see you again?"

"I'll be back. I enjoyed this visit and hopefully the more we talk, we can build our relationship back."

"I agree."

We both stood up to hug each other.

"I love you, Yah-Yah, and I'm proud of you."

It took a lot for me not to cry. I hadn't heard my mama say that since I was ten years old.

"I love you too, ma."

As I walked back to the car where Neca was waiting, my heart was content. I hated her for so long because she left me. Now that I had my own family, I see now she was gone but I was still taken care of. She provided financially because she couldn't be there physically.

"It must have went good 'cause you not mad and cussin'."

"It went real good. She looks so good if not better."

"Now ain't your black ass glad you came?"

"I am."

Neca dropped me off and I couldn't wait to get inside to tell Bash about my day. Kai was crying when I walked in and E'shon was running around like he was hyped off sugar.

"Hey baby! Don't worry 'bout the mess, I'm gon' clean it up."

"I know you are. You let them run you. How does a four-month old baby tell her daddy what to do?" I asked grabbing Kai from his arms.

"Baby, come sit down. I got to tell you something," Bash said nervously.

"What's wrong with her? She don't never cry like this." I checked her diaper but she was clean so I gave her my breast just to make her hush so I could hear Bash.

"Don't get mad at me but..."

"What Bash, damn?"

"My mama is going to be staying here until she heals."

I stood up from the sofa with Kai still attached to me. This was why I was still paying for my apartment just in case he lost his mind again. I went to our bedroom to get a few things so I could leave.

"Where you going?" Bash grabbed my bag.

"You know damn well I'm not staying in this condo with her. Why didn't you discuss this shit with me first to make sure I was cool with it?"

"Shit, I don't know. I thought you would have some compassion."

"Compassion? Fuck her! Whatever she gets, she deserves."

"Hold your damn voice down. She can hear you."

"I don't give a rat ass if she can hear me. We'll be back when that hoe leaves."

"Yahria, don't leave. We doing good."

"And we still gon' be good while I'm at my spot. You can come and chill or whatever but I'm not doing this crazy shit with y'all. That crazy bitch may try to kill me again."

"She ain't on that no more."

"Okay well, I'm out until her ugly ass out."

Bash wasn't expecting for me to take both of the kids but I didn't trust that hoe and my life was better when she wasn't around. I already texted Farrah and told her that me and the kids were at my place so she could watch them here. I had a flight in two weeks to go to New York for a fashion show and the last thing I needed was my kids being unsafe.

I gave both of them a bath, fed them and they were now down for the night. Bash had just texted me to open the door. This was the first time I was able to chill and watch television. I had my popcorn and wine ready with a blanket. Bash still had to sneak his grown ass up here so he was just walking in the door as I was getting comfortable on the sofa.

"Can I join you?"

"You don't have to ask me no shit like that."

"I'm just trying to make sure you ain't mad at me. I just got your lil' ass back liking me."

"I'm just mad you didn't talk to me first. That's why I didn't move my ass to your condo 'cause it's still yours and you have the say so just like I have the say so here. Me and your mama under the same roof is dangerous and you know that."

"I fucked that up. Don't hold that against me, it was the wrong judgment."

"Yep!"

"You got on my ass before I could ask you how did it go with your mama?"

"It was good."

"That's it?"

"Bash, I'm trying to watch a movie and you're interrupting me."

"I want to do a lil' more than interrupt you but I'll let you watch this weak ass movie."

Bash started taking off his clothes and climbed under the cover with me, laying his head on my stomach. If it wasn't for the sectional, half of his body would be hanging off the sofa.

"You not staying here tonight."

"You crazy as hell. I'm not 'bout to be away from y'all."

"So, what's the point of having your mama there and she by herself."

"Damn, I'll go home tomorrow."

Halfway through the movie Bash was snoring and slobbing on my damn stomach. I don't know why he was so damn tired because he didn't do shit but go to work and made sure everything else was done. Not wanting to move him, I fell asleep on the sofa with him until Kai and E'shon started screaming. Bash jumped up so fast he bowed me in the stomach.

E'shon was still learning how to talk so Bash was trying to get him to talk to figure out what was wrong with them. All he kept doing was pointing at the door. I got Kai settled in the room with me while Bash stayed with E'shon.

I woke up the next morning and made breakfast before Bash headed to shower and change to start his day.

"That boy tossed and turned all night. My back killing me."

"The kids hardly ever cry; I'm curious as to what scared him."

"He's at the age now where he's scared of everything. Ain't no telling what pop up on YouTube when he in there."

"You right 'bout that. Here, eat before you head home and deal with the devil."

"Come on with all that."

I threw my hands up and walked away. Bash would learn soon enough his mama was trash but it was going to have to hit him in the face for him to see it. Farah made it in enough time for me to stop by Big Ma house before I opened up shop. She pointed at the sofa while she sat on the phone.

"Guh, I knew that nigga wasn't no good. Uh huh! When his mama named his ass after a country that let me know they both was crazy. Yea, her ass just walked through the door. I'll talk to you later," Big Ma hung up the phone.

"What you gossiping 'bout now?"

"Gossiping 'bout your old nigga Egypt."

"Pharaoh, Big Ma."

"Chile, I don't give a damn what his name is right now. That nigga wanted for murder."

"Stop lying!"

"Shitttt, do it look like I'm lying?"

"Nah, he wouldn't do no shit like that. He was a lot of things but a killer ain't one."

"He probably did kill that damn girl. They still looking for her body and now her son without a mother."

I thought about the conversation we had before Pharaoh came back with her food at the carnival. She was really sweet and I thought she was a good fit for him. Pharaoh would never hurt anyone unless he was threatened and his girlfriend was way too timid to be a threat.

"It sound strange to me but hey, I guess we'll find out when the shit hit the fan. Now, on to you and your damn daughter keeping secrets," I stated.

"Whew, chile my chest hurtin'," she went to fanning herself.

"Big Ma quit playing with me."

"I'm from the hood so when I'm told to keep a secret I keep my mouth closed."

"Really? You could have told me that man was my damn daddy."

"You better bring that lil' ass voice down before I knock your voice box out your throat."

Kissing my teeth, I folded my arms and sat back on the sofa like a child. I didn't say nothing back because Big Ma would beat the hell out of me even at her age.

"You were too young to understand what was going on that's why I never said anything. It was plenty of times I wanted to tell you. All those times you would wake up before your alarm and you would see him roaming the halls, I wanted to tell you then but I couldn't. Now that you know, what are you going to do?"

"I want to see him. When is the last time you saw him?"

"It's been 'bout two weeks. He don't come 'round that much now. I told your mama it's 'cause you no longer in the house. He knew you were his child and once you moved out he would come and stare in your room."

"Does he talk?" I asked.

"Barely. He can though."

"I gotta find him."

"He hang out over there on your old block."

"A'ight, well I'm 'bout to head to work. I'll see you later and don't spend all of that on lottery," I gave her some money and kissed her on the cheek.

"Once you give it to me, I can do what I want."

"Okay, Big Ma."

I searched high and low for Tony but couldn't find him anywhere. I asked people had they seen him and nobody had seen him. Hopefully, he was somewhere safe.

15

Bash

MY LIFE WAS good right now and the last thing I needed was a bitch to be starting some shit that could make Yahria leave my ass for good. During the time she wasn't fuckin' with me, I had a few chicks that I smashed but I used protection. I've only slept with two women raw and that was Esha and Yahria, now I got a bitch calling up here making threats to tell my girl she pregnant. Any other time I wouldn't care but I lied to Yahria and told her I hadn't slept with anybody. Shit, I did what I had to do to get my damn girl back.

I didn't plan on staying open all day so I let my workers go home early just to handle this business with this chick. Hell, I didn't even know her name. I sent Yahria a text just see where she was at. I didn't need her ass popping up on me and showing out before knowing what was going on.

Me: Hey, you at work?
Bae: Why?

Me: I was just checking on you, damn.

Bae: Mmhhmm, what you 'bout to do?

I didn't respond because my accuser was walking her ass through the door. Once I saw her face, I remembered our night. She let me bust down with her and her homie. They were both trash but it kept me occupied while Yahria was having her tantrum. Normally, I was stingy with my dick for this reason alone.

"What's your name?" I asked her before she could walk up to me.

"It's sad you don't remember my name. Do you just randomly sleep with people?"

"I'm not answering any of your damn questions. The only reason you here is to piss on this stick and get the fuck on before my wife find you in here and beat your ass. Now, what's your name?"

"Tip."

"A'ight Tip. Take your ass in the bathroom and piss in this cup."

She snatched the cup away from me and walked towards the bathroom, trying to shut the door but I stopped it with my foot.

"Ain't nothing!"

"I can't have no privacy?"

"Ain't no privacy 'round this bitch. I done saw your chewed up ass pussy anyway. Pull them draws down and piss. The temperature better be right on that cup too."

She thought she was going to come in here and play me but I've seen it all when I was on the streets. As soon as she squatted, a condom full of piss fell in the toilet. This had to be the funniest shit I had ever experienced. She was so embarrassed, she pulled her pants up and walked out the bathroom.

"Next time, try that shit on a nigga that don't know the game with your dumb ass. Put a yoni egg up your shit to tighten that weak ass shit up."

"Fuck you nigga, your dick was trash anyway."

"Says a bitch that want to carry my baby."

Why I said that shit as Yahria was walking her ass through the door. My heart started racing so fast that I was getting lightheaded.

Her facial expression changed and she was no longer Yahria, she had turned into Yah-Yah.

"Repeat that shit again?" She walked up on Tip.

"Bash get your lil' pet."

Tip wrote a check that her ass couldn't cash. Yahria beat that girl ass so bad that I had to pull her off the girl. Tip left her wig and purse in the shop as she rushed to get her ass away from Yahria.

"Let me down! I asked your peasy head ass did you sleep with anybody and what did you tell me?"

"Yah-."

"What the fuck did you tell me, Bash?"

"I told you I didn't."

"Exactly, muthafucka!"

Yahria stormed off to the back and came back with a crowbar.

"Yahria, don't fuckin' try me."

"You tried me though, didn't you? It ain't nothing to tell the truth. Since you like to lie, lie to your gotdamn insurance company 'bout how I'm finna fuck your shit up." She raised the crowbar and busted the first showcase.

"Ayyee muthafucka! Don't make me beat your lil' ass in here," I told her.

She laughed before busting the next one. I had enough, I went to grab the crowbar but Yahria swung it at me hitting me in the side.

"You better leave me the fuck alone right now. The only reason I'm not beating your ass is 'cause it was while we were broken up. That hoe been calling me for weeks telling me she pregnant from you. I waited to see if your ass was gon' say something but you didn't so I connect our phones so I could see your damn text and shit. It don't cost shit to be honest to a muthafucka that got your best interest a heart," she said, throwing the crowbar down at my feet.

"Where you going?"

"The fuck away from you before I change my mind and beat your ass. Clean this shit up," Yahria stated.

Yahria walked out and climbed in her car like she didn't just leave me with a damn horror scene. Shattered glass was everywhere and jewelry was spread all over the floor.

"What kinda woman I done committed to?" I said out loud.

I tried my best to keep Yahria happy. If she ever got upset, you better believe she was fuckin' something up on site. No matter what she did, I wasn't going nowhere and this was all my fault. My girl was wise as fuck and she up on game a little more than me.

$$\sim$$

"I'm TIRED of sleeping on this damn sofa, Yahria," I told her from the other side of the door.

"Take your funky ass home then."

"I wasn't funky when I was eating your ass out last night," I kicked the door.

I been on the sofa for fourteen days. Yahria only talked to me when it was beneficial to her. Like last night, I had just came back from checking on my mama when I walked in Yahria's apartment. The kids were sleep and she wasn't in the living room so I assumed she was in her bedroom. She caught my ass trying to get a peek of her in the shower so she played that whole leave me alone game until I picked her ass up and sat her pussy on my face. She cool and content then until I was done and she put me out her room.

Yahria was punishing me for my shit I done apologized for over and over. I bought her ass a new car, she got several new purses, hell I even went and got her ass the new sewing machine she wanted that costed a grip but she was still treating me like the ugly step child. There was one more trick up my sleeve and if this didn't work, I was all out of options.

"Yahria! Open the door so I can kiss my kids before I go."

Her lil' short ass was talking shit all the way to the door. I was not surprised to see Kai sucking her mama titty because that's all she did. She was getting so fat she could barely wear any of her clothes. E'shon be so far up Yahria behind he forgot I even existed. I placed a kiss on his forehead while he laid there watching cartoons and then I kissed Kai.

"Can I give you a kiss, big baby?"

"Hell no! You said the kids."

"You need to cut this shit out, acting like a spoiled brat."

"I'm not acting. You thought it was cool to lie to me so I'm showing you how good my fall back game is."

"Answer this, if I would've told you that night that I smashed a few girls, what would your reaction have been?"

"I would've went across your head but I still would have felt better knowing you wasn't giving my dick away for real."

"Oh now it's your dick."

"Did you at least wear condoms?"

"Hell yea!"

"You were drunk that night at the club and I'm sure you was drinking all them others times so how do you know?"

"I don't drink, Yahria, and you know that. I ended up drunk that night 'cause your ass was over there in that section with all them niggas and you went to popping pussy like a stripper. Drinking was my only way of not catching a case. Again, I'm sorry for lying."

"I'll forgive you sometime this week. I'll let you know when."

"You childish as hell. Disconnect your phone from my shit, I got business moves to make."

"It better be business 'cause this time I'm driving to the ware-house and fuckin' up all your expensive ass cars."

"Yahria, I'm telling your lil' ass now if you do that I swear I'll beat your ass."

"Tuh! I guess we'll both find out."

"Crazy ass," I said walking out the bedroom.

YAHRIA WAS COMPLAINING about the space we were living in. Her apartment was super small but my condo was small too. We both had become accustomed to the big house and our split caused us both to downsize. If I planned on marrying her and having more kids, I had to put us in something bigger. Which is why I was about to close on this house not too far from the beach where I knew Yahria was gone be my girl.

The house wasn't as big as the house I once had but Yahria wasn't into material things; she just wanted to be comfortable. The six-bedroom house had five bathrooms with a big enough kitchen for Yahria and the master suite was massive. She would have her own closet so we wouldn't argue about where she was going to put all the stuff I constantly bought her. She wasn't aware that I had already purchased the house and was waiting to let her furnish it. There were a few issues that I had to iron out before I showed it to her.

"Subashtian, my nigga."

"Long time no see," I told him.

"You know how this life is, man."

"Shit, you know I know. So, what's up?" I asked him.

"The House is yours but I need a favor from you."

"Come on, you know I don't fuck with the streets unless my hand is forced."

"I'm sure when I tell you this, you'll be forced."

"I'm listening," I crossed my arms.

"There was a hit on you a few months ago. What if I told you I knew who it was?"

"I'm still listening."

"I had one of my spots robbed so I sent a few soldiers out to see what they could find out. I found it strange for someone would even try me unless the money was right."

"What this got to do with me? I'm not getting in no shit 'cause I got a family to take care of."

"Well, the guy that made the hit is the same for both of us."

"Listen, I killed the muthafucka that came at me. If that wasn't message enough not to come fuckin' with me, I don't know what else he need."

"Why not eliminate the problem? We go way back and I can't

trust no one with my life, like I can trust you. We started together so let's finish off a nigga that wanted us both out."

I looked over at my homeboy Markie and stared in his eyes to see how serious he was. We went way back to middle school days. It was his brother that made it easy for us to make money on the streets. Markie was the man now since his brother's death; he was so normal nobody ever knew and that's why I rocked with him so long. We did so much shit together that we had no choice but to hold each other down. If either of us talked, we were looking at football numbers.

"I got you, bruh, but we got to sit down and talk this shit out so I can make it back to my girl and kids."

"You know I wouldn't let shit happen to you. When I'm gon' meet this chick?"

"Soon, nigga. I appreciate the steal on the house, though."

"Just an early engagement gift for your soft ass. I thought you had it bad for Esha."

"Mannnn, Esha did have me but Yahria helped a nigga come out that depression and her sex so much better than Esha."

"I can't wait to meet her 'cause your ass done went soft."

We talked a little longer before we parted ways. I had to figure out how to surprise Yahria with the house. She hated surprises but her expression always made me happy and let me know I was doing my job. Before heading to the condo, I went back to check on the kids and Yahria. She was on the phone talking to Neca about her upcoming trip to New York. Pulling my phone out my pocket, I called my mama to see if she needed anything before I got there. My body was sore so all I had planned was sleeping in my bed.

Walking up behind Yahria, I wrapped my arms around her small waist. She was being stingy with her pussy but she was gon' give that shit up. She tried to push me off but she should know by now she couldn't do shit to me unless she was having one of her rage moments. I pulled her panties to the side and played with her pearl. It didn't take her long to get wet like I liked it.

"Tell her you'll call her back," I whispered in her ear.

She shook her head no as she kept talking.

"I'm warning you now, Yahria, once I put this bitch in, I ain't showing your lil' ass no mercy."

She ignored me again. Both the kids were down for a nap so I had to make this quick. I pulled my pants down and pulled my shit out, placing it at her warm opening. She was playing hard as I slowly entered her fold, trying to get her adjusted to my size. After a few sticky pumps she started stuttering, making me laugh.

"I told you to get off the phone. Hang up!" I told her as I started thrusting deeper in her.

Her legs were getting weak on me so I knew I was hitting that shit right. She laid the phone down and arched her back. I let her grind her hips while I picked up the phone.

"Aye, Neca look here. I'm trying to fuck her real good before the kids wake up. She'll call your ass back," I said before hanging up on her.

Yahria was grinding so good on the dick, I let her ass catch her first nut just like that. She was getting weak in me again so I had to change positions.

"Wrap your legs around me."

I walked her over to the back of the sofa and pulled out of her because I wanted to see her face as I stroked her. Yahria flipped over so I could see her face. She grabbed my dick and guided it back in her as she moaned out in pleasure.

"I love the fuck outta you girl. You better not ever leave me. You hear me?"

"Yes!"

"I need you to make that shit slippery for me one more time. Can you do that for daddy?" I asked her, playing with her clit.

Her body responded immediately. I smiled down at her as her body shivered and released the thick white substance on my dick. Raising her legs, I pulled her down so she was hanging off the sofa. I wanted all pussy for this nut.

"Squeeze my shit and you better not let it go until I bust this nut."

Pushing her legs back as far as they would go, I pushed in and out of her until I couldn't hold on any longer. Yahria was definitely pregnant after this session. I had to be careful with her ass because she had me so wrapped around her finger that I let her get away with a lot of shit.

"You gon' let me get up or you just gon' stand there looking off in space?" Yahria broke me from my trance.

"I was just sitting here thinking 'bout how I'm gon' kill your ass if you try me with some bullshit."

"Move your ass out the way. You the only one 'round here with extracurricular activities."

"Don't start that," I pulled my pants up and helped her down.

"You going home today?"

"If you ask me that one more time. Wherever y'all at, that's my home. Am I going to check on my mama, yes I am."

"Well you need to take E'shon to see his mama 'cause I'm tired of her hitting me up in my DM's."

"Fuck her! Why she ain't called me? My number ain't changed."

"Shit, I don't know; that's your baby mama."

"And I'm y'all baby daddy," I teased.

"You ain't my baby daddy, we just got the same baby," Yahria burst out laughing.

"You ain't shit. I'll be back and I'm not sleeping on the sofa."

"Go home!"

I kissed Yahria before walking out the door. I don't care what nobody said about me and my girl; we were straight and wasn't nothing coming between what we build together.

16

P haraoh

"DADDY I WANT you to come home," Cissy whined in the phone.

"Baby, I will as soon as I get some things cleared. Daddy loves you and take care of your sister." I hung up the phone before the tears fell from my eyes.

If I could go back to the day I met Kelly, I would walk away from that table and go do my time for drugs. She fucked my whole life up in months. I been constantly on the run and I was getting tired of buying burner phones just to talk to my daughter. There had to be a way to clear my name from this shit but the news said my bloody fingerprints were at the scene. The look on Taelor's son face and her ex-husband broke my heart.

The day I dropped Kelly ass off to have her baby, I left thinking I could take a shower and go back up there. Before I could step out the door, there was two police officers at the door. A nigga from the streets automatically felt some type of way when the police popped up to their crib but something told me that Kelly sent them. I left my phone in the house along with my car keys and dipped out the back door. The first place I could think of was Kesh spot but knowing Kelly she would have sent them there so I left the state and came all the way to New York.

I only did my moving around at night so no one would notice me. My funds couldn't be touched because they would know where I was so I did shit that I saw the homeless do to make a little cash. That was beneath me so I jacked a few niggas until I was able to rent a hole in the wall apartment. The landlord didn't ask for nothing but his money which worked out in my favor. Every night I dealt with roaches and rats but it was better than going to jail for some shit I didn't do.

After throwing the burner phone away, I walked down to the Chinese restaurant that I frequent before going back home. It was cheap and I could eat off of it for days at a time. Before I walked into the restaurant there was a billboard with a flyer on it about a fashion show. What caught my eye was the picture of Yah-Yah as one of the designers. The address was way in the Manhattan area and there was only one way to get over there. I had a lot to do before tomorrow so instead of getting something to eat, I went and sat on the block like a crackhead so I could hit a lick to buy something decent to put on.

By morning, I counted almost four thousand dollars. That was enough to buy me something to wear and pay for transportation over to Manhattan. Taking my chance in the daylight, I went to a few spots downtown and grabbed something to wear before showering and catching my ride so I could be seated before the show started. I kept my shades on and made sure I sat in the very back where the lights were dim.

I had to see her and let her know that I didn't do this. Whatever happened to me after this, I was content with because I was tired of running. I let my greed for money and my love for Yah-Yah knock me off my game. Kelly manipulated me into thinking getting Yah-Yah back was going by to be easy. She had moved on to someone that was truly down for her and she deserved it. I dogged her for so long it was time for her to shine. This was always one of her dreams and it felt good to sit here and watch it come alive.

The show was over so I slipped out and walked around back in hopes to run into Yah-Yah. I was shocked that she traveled without her nigga but then I heard Neca's voice. She was talking with one of the girls in the back while she waited for Yah-Yah to finish taking pictures. I didn't move until I heard her voice. Yah-Yah and Neca screamed and hugged out of excitement. My cousin was a true friend, I had to respect their relationship and now I realized why they went so hard for each other.

"Yah-Yah," I said lowly so I couldn't be noticed.

Her and Neca turned around and looked like they seen a ghost.

"Can I have a few moments with my friend?" Yah-Yah asked the crew that was following her.

When the area was cleared, I walked out so they could see me. I was a little embarrassed by my appearance but that faded just as quick as it came.

"Pharaoh, what the fuck is going on? You are all over the news back home," Yah-Yah stated.

"You know I didn't do that shit. I loved that girl and I had planned on spending the rest of my life with her."

"What happened? Obviously something happened that night 'cause she's dead."

"Kelly did that shit."

"That bitch! Yah-Yah, we got to kill that hoe," Neca paced.

"I ended up staying with Taelor that night after we made love."

"Don't need those details," Yah-Yah stopped me.

"I spent the night. My phone kept going off so I shut it off and went to piss when the lights went out. I cut them back on and Kelly crazy ass was standing there looking innocent as fuck. She stabbed that girl so many times, I don't know how I slept through it."

"This shit is crazy!"

"She then made me help her get rid of the body."

"Raoh! What the fuck! Do you know how much time you can get for that?"

"Listen, I saw you on the billboard and wanted to let you know I didn't do the shit. I'm sure I'll get caught eventually 'cause of all the connects Kelly got. As long as y'all know I'm innocent, I'm good."

"I don't even know where to begin to get your name cleared."

"Don't worry 'bout that shit. I'll be straight either way. Neca, check on my girls for me from time to time and make sure they straight. Let my mama them know, I didn't do this shit."

I didn't wait for them to say anything else. It was time for me to relocate again before the corner boys were after me.

17

Yah-Yah

"BITCH, WHAT YOU GON' do? Are you gon' tell Bash or we just go in that bitch kill her ass and leave?" Neca questioned.

Both of us were a nervous wreck since running into Pharaoh in New York. That was three days ago and we were still plotting what we wanted to do. Bash was gone on a trip and was expected to return tonight. I had already sent Farrah home to get some rest. Neca wouldn't let me stay alone now that she knew Kelly ass wasn't normal in the head.

"What am I supposed to tell that man when he come home? Don't you think that's a bit strange?"

"Hell nah! You tell that nigga his mama is a fuckin' murderer and you don't want to be 'round that hoe."

"I'm not worried 'bout her bothering with me since I fucked her up at the reveal party. I was pregnant and out of breath then, I'm back to normal now."

"All I need is the word and we'll go kill her ass. All we need is some gloves and shit."

"I'm sure you need more than that. I'll let you know if I tell him or not. In the meantime, you gone on back to your big house in the hills, Bash will be home tonight."

"You sure? I don't want to leave y'all until he gets here."

"Neca, we good. She got to get pass the doorman."

"Chile, his ass ain't nothing but a big flirt. That's why he tried to take Bash to court when y'all started back going together. He thought he was gon' shoot his shot."

"He's pretty strict 'bout who he lets up here. Trust me, I'll be fine, now go."

Neca grabbed her stuff and looked at me for assurance before leaving. I still needed to wash clothes and get E'shon's stuff together because he was spending a few days with his mama. Bash finally was able to move past Esha disappearing, leaving him with all the parenting responsibilities. With my help, I talked Bash into letting him stay with her for two days just to see how it went. She wanted to talk to me but I wasn't quite ready to see her ass yet. She caused a lot of hell in my relationship and now she was laid up with my number one enemy. I couldn't trust neither of them hoes right now.

"Bash, I'm tired so I'm 'bout to hang up."

"Dang you can't talk to your man until I get on my flight?"

"We been on the phone for two hours you ain't flying out no time soon with bad weather."

"I miss y'all. You can't go out of town without us no more."

"Same thing goes for you. You never told me what you were doing."

"Business, baby. Just business."

"It better be business. You know I'll fuck all y'all up."

"Mannn, there you go. You know when I'm with you ain't nobody getting this dick. I'm faithful baby."

"You better be 'cause I ain't taking you back no more."

"Your ass ain't going nowhere. We got kids together, you'll always have to see me."

"Bye Bash!"

"Bye, baby. I love you and I'll see you in a few hours."

"Love you too," I told him.

It was damn near midnight and he had me up talking on the phone like we were teenagers. It was cute, though, and I was glad he thought to call me instead of entertaining another female. Kai would be up for a feeding in about two hours, so I slipped in bed and went to sleep.

The sound of Kai crying through the monitor woke me up. Without looking at the time or anything, I groggily walked to her without looking at my surroundings. My body was tired and all I wanted to do was grab her and take her back to my bed to feed her. Between her teething and me trying to wean her, Kai was becoming a little diva.

"I'm coming, Kai."

I looked at E'shon's room and his room door was still slightly closed. Usually, I let them sleep in the same room but Bash was trying to break him from being so dependent and scared. He had a monitor in his room so I grabbed Kai and went back in my room. Once she latched on, I went back to sleep.

"Door! Door!"

My eyes fluttered open to see E'shon standing in the side of the bed tapping my shoulder.

"What is it E'shon?"

"Door...door!"

"Ain't nobody at the door. Come on and get in the bed with us," I went to reach for him but he took off running.

"Boy, get your butt in here and get in the bed." I eased Kai from under me and fixed my clothes so I could go get him. If I didn't, my house would be a mess when I got up.

"Door!" E'shon stood there pointing at my front door standing wide open.

I snatched him and shut the door and locked it. Before I went to sleep, I thought I put the chain on the door but then I thought about Bash coming home in the middle of the night so I didn't put it on. I was so terrified that someone had been in my house with my kids and I was too tired to even know it. I picked E'shon up and went in my room and locked us in there.

Bash still hadn't made it home and now I was worried. I turned the television on cartoons before I picked up the phone to call Bash but it went straight to voicemail. Now I could see why Big Ma kept her two guns at all times. She had one in her purse and the other on the side of her bed. First thing tomorrow, I was going to purchase one because I refuse to be afraid in my own house. It was a hard task but I got E'shon back to sleep. I laid there awake as the sun came up. An hour later, my phone started ringing with Bash name displaying.

"Hello."

"Come take the chain off the damn door."

I was afraid to come out the room. What if someone was on the other side of the door as Bash couldn't get in here to save us? Hell, I wasn't about to live like this. Snatching the door open, I walked quickly up the hall to open the door for Bash.

"You okay?" He asked, dropping his bags at the door.

"Yea, I'm good."

"You don't look good."

"I'm tried that's all. I've been up all night with E'shon."

"What he do? I bet you got him in the bed with you don't you. I swear, Yahria, you got to let him grow up and stop babying him."

"First of all, he's almost two and second, someone broke in here last night and if he didn't come wake me up I don't know what would've happened."

"Fuck you mean someone broke in here?" Bash started looking around making sure nothing was missing. "Are y'all okay? I'm not leaving anymore."

"We're good! They are both in the bed sleep."

"Okay well, I'm 'bout to wake they ass up. You moving out today."

"And going where? Damn sure not where your mama at."

"Shut up sometimes and do as I say."

Bash stood there in his all black looking like a real boss. I'm not sure what he did while I was gone but I don't think I had ever seen him dress the way he was dressed this morning. Even the look in his eyes was off but I wasn't going to push the issue. I trusted him with our life, and even if we weren't together, he would still be the one I called if something happened.

Bash knew I was about to go in on him as soon as he pulled up to his condo. That's why he hopped his ass out the car real fast and grabbed Kai and E'shon before I could slap the shit out of him. The fact that I told him I didn't want to come here with his mama was disrespectful and meant he didn't care about my feelings or safety. This bitch killed a woman that didn't even know she existed and had Pharaoh running for his damn life.

"Bash, I'm not going in there and don't take my damn kids in there," I told him.

"Girl, get out the car and bring your ass on. I would rather have y'all here than over there and you don't know who breaking in the damn apartment. It was probably one of your old niggas."

"I'm not playing with you, right now."

"Look, my mama ain't even here. She ain't been here in a minute and she probably not coming back. Now, bring your ass on."

I got out but if she popped up while I was here, somebody was going to die and damn sure wasn't going to be me. She wasn't there when we got inside so I went on about my regular routine like she was never there. Bash came into the kitchen while I was cooking and dropped a set of keys on the counter.

"What is that?"

"The key to your new spot. I want you to go today and look at it so you can start getting it furnished. I want to be out this condo by the end of the month."

"Bash, what did you do to get this?" I asked.

"What the hell you talking 'bout?"

"What did you have to go out of town for? I've been in the streets all my life and I know when some shit done went down. I wasn't going to say anything but I don't want to raise these kids by myself 'cause you done something stupid for a house."

"Man, I got money to buy what the hell I want. I don't have to do shit for it either. You don't have to worry 'bout me leaving you with the kids. The only way I'm gone lay down and do some time is for y'all. As soon as I find out who been in your shit, I will be handling that, though."

"We are fine, Bash, so there's no need to go and start no shit. But you still hadn't answered my question."

"Yahria, don't worry 'bout what I went and did. We good and that's all you need to know," he kissed me before going to sit in the living room with the kids.

"YEP, bitch you need to marry him today," Neca said walking through the house. "It ain't as big as the other house but this shit is nice as fuck. I can put a whole living suit in y'all bedroom and a California king bed."

"I don't even know where to start with decorating."

"I'm sure your ass will come up with something. What I want to know is did you tell him 'bout his mama."

"No, I haven't said anything."

"I talk to Pharaoh the other day. He's good but he's thinking 'bout turning himself in 'cause he's all out of money and he can't keep robbing niggas for money to survive."

"I hate this happened to him but he did side with that hoe to break me and Bash up. What did he expect to happen when you link up with a damn snake?"

"You got a point. I told him to do whatever he felt was right."

"It's good to see y'all working on y'all relationship."

"Nah, we ain't that cool. I was with Gip and he called for a few minutes."

"So, you and Gip serious, huh?"

"I wouldn't say that. I can't settle down with a nigga just yet. You know I can't be faithful. I'm just like the niggas out here, the only difference is I get paid for my time. I be damn if you gon' waste my damn time. I'm 'bout to open another salon on another side of town."

"You definitely be getting these niggas."

"They been doggin' females for years until they run across a bitch like me. I may let them lick the cat after it's said and done. Everybody thinks I sleep with majority of the men they see me with, but I only sleep with about three percent. Most of them don't even get to sniff it. I get what I want and block they ass from contacting me."

"I swear you cold with it."

"Until somebody treating me like Bash do you, I'm gon' continue to dog em' out. Just call be the female version of a pimp."

We both laughed as we walked back through the house to leave. I took all of this in and smiled. Bash was always doing something to keep me happy. Because I never asked him for anything, he made sure I had more than enough of everything. I stood outside with Neca for a few minutes and talked before we parted ways and I headed to Big Ma's house to check on her. Bash was spending time with the kids today which gave me a much-needed break but I was afraid of how the house was going to look when I got back. He had no control over his kids and let them do what they wanted.

"You came over here just in time. Come look at this shit," Big Ma waved me over to the television.

The news was displaying a car in a high speed chase in the streets of Houston. I sat on the sofa and tried to see what was so important about watching the police chasing a nigga through the streets but I hadn't read the small caption at the bottom of the screen.

"Is that who I think it is?" I asked.

"Yep, what the hell he doing in Texas? I'm so glad you broke it off with that damn boy. He done lost all his mind."

I swallowed hard. This wasn't going to end well and I didn't want to watch it any longer so I cut it off.

"You don't need to watch that. It's more to the story than you know. For his sake, I hope he just pull over before he hurts someone."

"Did you just turn my damn television off? Bash bought me this, not you. Now, get your ass out of the way. He deserves everything he's getting right now. He should not have killed that girl."

"He didn't kill her, Big Ma. He was in love with her."

"Chile, gone," she waved me off.

"Kelly killed that girl and framed him."

Big Ma's mouth fell open. If Pharaoh died today, then I was going to be the one to put his truth out there and I didn't care how anybody felt about it.

"She did what?"

"It's a long story that I don't care to get into but Pharaoh was sleeping with Kelly but moved on and I guess she wasn't having it. That's the short version."

"Damn! Well, he made his bed and it's time to lay his ass down in it. I still don't feel an ounce of pity for this nigga. I'm sorry, baby."

I was sick to my stomach so I didn't stay. I left and headed home a little earlier than expected. I'm sure Neca would be calling me telling me the end results of what happened. Pharaoh should have never got involved with Kelly then this wouldn't be happening.

"Bash, why the hell is it shit everywhere? I haven't been gone but a few hours."

"I was gon' have it cleaned up before you got back but you back all early and shit. What you doing back so soon? I thought I told you to go to the damn spa or something."

"I don't feel good so I'm going to lay down."

"You pregnant?"

"Bash, please don't start that shit. No, I'm not pregnant. I've been taking my birth control and plan B pills."

"Plan B? So, you taking hoe pills now?"

"I've always took them, even when I was with Pharaoh."

"I ain't him."

"Okay, I don't want to argue."

"Don't take them no damn more and I mean that shit from the bottom of my heart."

I went in the room and closed the door. Pulling the cover over my head, I shut my eyes and tried to think about something other than the shit that I saw on the news. The fear of his death and him leaving his girls hurt me. I couldn't even think about leaving my kids. Before I closed my eyes, I said a quick prayer for him.

"Baby, wake up. Yahria! Get up."

"What's wrong."

"You saw this shit?"

"Saw what?"

"Your nigga out there showing his ass, running from the police and shit for killing that girl."

"You sound like a female gossiping."

"Shit, it's all over the news and shit. This ain't no damn gossip and if you ever come at me like that again, I'll choke the shit out of you."

I turned the television with my stomach in knots, not knowing what I was about to see when it came on. It ended just like I thought it would. Pharaoh was shot over sixteen times after his car hit a curb and crashed into a light pole. He was already dead from the impact of the crash but they still riddled his body with bullets. I shut the television off and slid back down in the bed. My heart was hurting for his family. I picked up the phone to call Neca.

"Yahriaaa, why they do that?"

"Neca, calm down."

"They didn't have to do him like that. We weren't close but damn, he did not deserve that shit."

"I know. I know. Where are you? Do you need me to come to you?"

"No, I'm fine. I'm going to my mama house so we can go to his mama house."

"Are you sure?"

"I'm good girl. I'll call you back in a few to let you know what I find out."

"Okay."

Bash stood at the door staring at me before walking away. I didn't need any beef in my house but I was concerned about the situation. To keep shit down, I did get out the bed to make sure Bash wasn't on any bullshit.

18

Kelly

THE NEWS WAS DEVASTATING and I couldn't help but cry and laugh at the situation. From the time he left me at the hospital, I just knew he was going to the police on me so I had to beat him to it. Since my sister wasn't talking to me since our last family Thanksgiving, I couldn't call her so I called her husband which was Bash's father and he sent someone to the rescue. I wasn't expecting Pharaoh to run the way he did but when you're innocent, you don't want to sit in a jail cell and wait for death to knock on your door.

Everything in my house was packed and ready for the moving guys to pick up in the morning. It was best for me to get the hell out of dodge before some shit popped off and there was no telling what all damage Pharaoh had done before he went on that high speed chase. Being out in public was starting to make me paranoid but I knew it was karma slowly creeping up on me to give me what was due for all the evil things I've done. There was no regret in my heart for any of them. Everything that I've done, I had a reason for it.

Disrespect was not tolerated and if I felt it in any kind of way, you had to be eliminated. There was still one person that I wanted gone but my son had her guarded like a damn jailhouse prisoner. I had two chances to kill her but my grandchildren stopped me. Yes, it was me that was in her house. Not once but twice. Yahria was young and careless. What woman leaves the chain off the door when you know it's just you and children in the home? A few deep throats for the doorman and I had a permanent key to Yahria's apartment.

The first night I went in, Bash was there so I knew I couldn't do anything. The second time was last night. I went into her room as she slept but Kai was awake and looking dead at me. Her eyes were so piercing that it sent chills down my spine. I thought if I turned the television off so I wouldn't see her eyes, I could get the job done but even in the dark, her big eyes continued to stare through my soul. There was no connection between us because I refused to be a part of her life due to Yahria. I decided to wait it out until E'shon caught me coming out of the room. Panic set in and I ran out.

Yahria had been teaching him how to talk and I didn't know just how much he knew at the moment so I didn't chance it. Now, I was headed to see Bash before I left town for good. I wasn't about to tell him that so he could become suspicious or anything. The sound of E'shon's feet running on the side of the door should have made me turn around but to see Yahria opening the door to walk out made my feet move towards the door.

"Excuse me," I squeezed by her, making sure to brush her just a little bit.

"Ma, what you doing here?" Bash asked.

"I was coming to grab the rest of my things. Especially, since you've moved your family back in here."

Yahria closed the door back and stood there with her arms folded like she was waiting on something to pop off.

"What you mean? They were here before you. Yahria moved out briefly 'cause of y'all beef."

"Well, you can tell your girl she can go wherever she was going before I walked in here. She don't have to stand there and bodyguard shit in here."

"You came to start shit didn't you?" Bash asked.

"Nah, I came to get my stuff. She the one standing there staring at me."

"Yahria, would you go and get the stuff for dinner tonight please baby," Bash begged.

"Only 'cause you asked but I'm taking Kai with me now that she's here," Yahria stated.

"Why? I can take care of my daughter. She is my mama grandchild."

"Nope, she ain't part of me," I said.

"Fuck you, you dirty bitch. I don't want my daughter to be a part of your ugly ass anyway. Don't think I don't know what the fuck you did but it's all good, hoe. Your time coming," Yahria gave me an evil grin.

"Bitch, you don't know shit 'bout me. Get your broke ass out of here before I beat your ass this go around."

Yahria gave her daughter back to Bash and squared up like she was ready to throw the first punch.

"See son, you can't take the hood out of this hoe. She ready to fight right in front of your kids."

"Ma, get your shit and get on. And Yahria, take Kai and go to the store and bring your lil' ass back."

"Door!" E'shon pointed at me.

Yahria turned around quickly and stared at me.

"Come here, E'shon," Bash called out to him.

Yahria shook her head at me and continued to smile before she walked out the door. She knew something. I just didn't know how much she knew and I wasn't sticking around to find out. I walked to the back room to get the things I left here.

"Ma, why you always starting with her? I'm trying to keep peace in my house and every time you come 'round it's some shit."

"I don't start with her. It's clear we don't like each other so I try to stay away from her. I didn't know her ass was here. If I would've known, I would have waited or never came."

"I'm not trying to keep her away; all I'm saying is speak and keep it moving."

"Don't worry; I'm 'bout to be out of your hair for good so you can live your life. That is what you want, right?"

"Yea, that's what I want."

"Okay, then your wish is granted. I'm done and I won't bother you again."

"What happened to your hand?" Bash grabbed my hand and examined it.

"I hit it on the door. It's fine," I snatched away. "No need to be concerned with me."

"Ma, I'm not asking you to just never come 'round. I'm asking for you to keep the peace. You are older than her and you set her off; it's never her bothering you first. She's been respectful and you've still been rude. I don't blame her for not even fuckin' with you at this point."

"I'm in the way so I'm removing myself."

"Okay, if that's what you want. I wanted you to be 'round when I propose to Yahria."

"Propose? You can't marry her. Esha is supposed to be your wife and she's over there confused laid up with a damn woman not taking care of her son."

"And that is why I'm marrying Yahria. She did what no other woman would do. She loves my son just like she had him. She not childish when Esha calls to talk to him and the only reason he ain't went over there yet is 'cause I just got back in town. But he will go and spend time with her tomorrow."

"Do what you want, Subashtian. I stand on my word when I say she's going to drag you down and then take everything."

"I know her better than you do and she's the most loyal chick I've ever been with."

"Did she tell you she was with Pharaoh while she was in New York? While you trying to marry her you better make sure that little girl is yours. You know how that girl was 'bout that nigga. I wouldn't be surprised if she didn't sleep with both of y'all."

From the expression on my son's face, I knew he had no clue. I exaggerated a little bit but I'll be gone by the time she got back and now it was her word against mine.

"I guess you didn't know that. Anyway, good luck on that proposal son."

I walked out the door before he could say anything else to me. Fuck him and everything connected to him. I tried my best to raise him to not need any other woman but me or the woman I placed in his life. He couldn't do that so I didn't give a fuck about him at this moment.

19

Yahria

"WHERE YOU BEEN for four damn hours?" Bash jumped in my face as soon as I walked in the house.

"What the hell wrong with you? I went to go and check on my friend and then I went to the store. I was giving your mama time to get the hell on."

"You got some shit you need to tell me?"

"If you don't get these groceries out of my hand or your daughter. You can't even be a man 'cause you starting shit that I don't know what you talking 'bout."

Bash grabbed Kai to lay her down on the sofa but he was right back in my face while I pulled the stuff out the bag.

"What is it I'm supposed to be telling you?" I asked.

"What you did in New York?"

"I worked, what the fuck you mean."

"Have I cussed you, Yahria."

"Umm, yes! As soon as I walked back through the door."

"Is Kai my child, Yahria?"

I laughed because he had flipped on me. That damn Scorpio was something serious in him. He was fine and then flip when you don't act like he wants you to.

"Yahria, don't laugh right now 'cause I'm trying not to wrap my hands 'round your lil' ass throat."

"You can try and do it, Bash. One of us won't make it out the kitchen today. You know I don't play that dumb ass shit. Now I don't know what done came over you while I was gone but maybe you need to leave and come back with your head on straight."

"My head on straight. I asked you what you did in New York and you ain't being truthful. Then I ask you is Kai mine and you laugh."

"I'm laughing 'cause you dumb as fuck. Do you see that black ass baby laying on that sofa? You know damn well she belongs to you and the only thing I did was carry her ass. Now if you having issues with being her daddy let me know so I can go find someone that don't mind, just like I don't mind being a mama to your son."

"Is it a problem?"

"Shit, you the one in here with your chest puffed out asking 'bout my baby and she five months old now. You should've asked me that when I had her and you was shacked up with that gay hoe. You're welcome to test her but just know if you do, I'm leaving your strong neck ass and we not coming back. Ever!"

I walked away from him before I got violent. That's why I hated when she came around because she always stirred the damn pot and disappeared like she hadn't done shit.

"Were you laid up with Pharaoh while you were in New York?" Bash asked.

I stopped cleaning up E'shon's mess and glared at Bash.

"Did I see Pharaoh? Yes, I did. It was only for a few minutes. He came to the show to show his support. I mean he knew this was something I've always wanted."

"It's crazy how you left that part of your trip out when I asked you how it went."

"Just like you left out all the damn parts of you trip. Now what?" I crossed my arms. "You the one fuckin' Bash not me. You tell me what you did and I'll tell you what me and him talked 'bout."

When he walked out the room, I knew his ass was up to no good while he was gone. It was cool because as soon as I found out what it was, he knew I was gone beat his ass. E'shon was on his tablet watching YouTube as I cleaned up.

"E'shon, who is door?"

"Door," he replied.

He didn't know how to say his grandma name but I had a feeling it was her that was in my apartment that night. He saw her and didn't know how to articulate it. Once I finished cooking dinner I was heading back to my apartment and tried to figure out how she was able to have access without me giving the doorman permission.

Bash and I didn't speak for the rest of the day. We sat at the table and ate in silence. He didn't think I noticed how he was treating Kai. She was wanting some of his attention but he was ignoring her like a complete asshole. It don't matter how mad I was with him, I would never treat E'shon any different.

"So, you don't see your daughter?" I asked him.

"Oh, she mine now?"

"Bitc-." I bit my tongue and clenched my fist. "I've never treated your son different and he for sure ain't mine. But you can keep ignoring her with your pussy ass."

"Watch your mouth right now before you piss me off."

"Nigga, you already done pissed me off. You let your mama run your fuckin' life nigga. Go fuck her dumb ass, she may like that shit with her weird ass. As a matter fact you weird too with your ugly ass. Take care of your son on your own or go take him to his damn mama so she can confuse the fuck out of him. Fuckin' mama boy ass nigga." I threw my damn drink at his ass and got up from the table.

My mouth would cut anyone and I did regret some of the shit I said after it was already out of my mouth but he wasn't about to treat her like that because of some shit his mama came in here and started and he too damn blind to see. We had to separate for the night or we were going to end up fighting. Bash never hit me but by the time I finished calling him a bitch ass nigga, he'll want to fight me.

"Fuck you going?"

"To mind my business with *my* child."

"Yahria, get your ass back in here and talk."

"Talk? Nigga you came at me and I don't like to feel threatened."

"I haven't threatened you yet."

It was funny how calm he was as the tea still dripped from his face. He was mad but still calm which is why I had to hit his ass before he got a hold of me because only crazy muthafuckas acted like Bash. But I was Yah-Yah and I did what I wanted to do so I walked out with my daughter on my hip.

I got on the elevator and closed the door as Bash came running up to the door. While he was chasing us, he was leaving E'shon in the house by himself. I hit the alarm on his Audi because my car was still at my apartment. I quickly put Kai in her car seat and strapped her in right as Bash was walking out of the building. I hated that he was in shape. His ass took ten flights of stairs like it was a walk in the park.

"Yahria don't get in that damn car and leave."

I backed away as he walked up to the car. All of his muscles were flexed as he hit the hood of the car.

"Yahria if I have to come get you...okay!" He yelled as I pulled off.

Bash's ass was dysfunctional like his mama. I went to Big Ma house to drop Kai off before I headed back to my apartment. If Bash showed up there, we could fight or whatever he wanted to do when he got there as long as my daughter wasn't there to witness how crazy we were.

"What the hell you doing? And why Bash calling me back to back? I'm too old to be fuckin' 'round with y'all crazy asses now."

"Fuck Bash! Fuck his mama! Hell fuck everybody connected to him but Kai."

"Okay, where you going?"

"I got to run to my apartment real quick. Don't let Bash take my baby nowhere since he don't think she his."

"Bash need to cut it out."

"His sorry ass mammy put that in his head."

"Well when you calm down. I got to tell you something."

"I'm calm but I'll be back in 'bout an hour. She got milk still in your freezer?"

"Yea she good. Plus, Big Ma got some greens and corn bread for that baby."

"Don't feed my baby that."

"Get your ass on. I been raising children all my damn life. You grew up on it so shut the hell up and let me tend to my great grand-baby while you go out there and do what you do. Gone!"

"I'm not going to do anything but see something."

"Well go see something and get out of my face. Trying to tell me what I can and can't do with Kai," she mumbled.

I jumped back in Bash car and headed to my place. Because I was smarter than Bash thought I was, I didn't park his car in my other parking spot. I used someone else's and walked to my build-ing. The doorman was sitting there looking at a magazine when I walked in.

"Could you tell me if anyone else has a key to my apartment?"

"How am I supposed to tell you that?" He stated with an attitude.

"Look here bitch, you worked the other night when a muthafucka came in my house. If you don't want to lose your job, I suggest you get to talking."

"I don't have a clue what you are talking about."

"Okay, you want to play this game. As a tenant here I can request to get the cameras pulled. I'm sure you wouldn't want that."

He became nervous as he looked around and back at me. His nose started to sweat and he was about to spill the beans until Bash came and scooped me up. It didn't take much because I was only about a buck forty-five.

"Bash put me the fuck down right now."

"I told you not to damn leave didn't I? Where the fuck Kai at?"

"Why you worried 'bout it bitch."

Bash slammed my back up against the wall in the elevator.

"Stop with the gotdamn name calling. Now, listen to what the fuck I got to say and you can feel however the fuck you want to feel after this."

"Put me down and then I'll listen."

Bash let me down but still hemming me in the corner. I looked at the number in the elevator and was glad it was about to stop ion my floor. The doors flew open so I stared up at Bash to see if we were going to stand here or go inside to talk.

"Bring your ass on."

Following behind him, I looked up at the cameras and pointed to let that weak ass doorman know, I was coming back for his ass. Bash unlocked the door and let me in first before walking in and shutting the door. He paced back and forth like he was trying to think of the right words to say.

"I'm sorry for questioning you 'bout Kai. I was acting like a jealous ass boyfriend when I found out you were in New York with him."

"I wasn't with him! How hard is that for you to understand?"

"Damn Yahria, listen! I know she's mine, okay. I wanted to see if you would be truthful with me. I'll admit that I let my mama put shit in my head, that's my fault. As far as what I was doing out of town, I still don't want to tell you. But if it will release some of the tension between us then I'll tell you."

"Don't do that reverse psychology shit on me. I hate when y'all cheat and then try to make it to where we won't ask y'all shit. Yep, I want to know."

"Me and my best friend killed somebody. Our lives were threatened so we went to handle it. There, you happy?"

"Bash why would you stand here and still lie to my face?"

"What did I lie 'bout?"

"You don't have that in you to kill nobody. Well, besides the man that tried to rob you but hell, anybody could do that when they are scared."

"You have me sadly mistaken, Yahria. You don't know me like you think you do. That part of my life is gone until I feel threatened."

I searched his eyes to find some truth in what he was saying. Bash didn't flinch or blink while I stared at him.

"If you don't want to be with me 'cause I still got some street shit in me, I understand but I can promise you that I would never put you or the kids in harm's way. If anything I'll handle the problem before you have to."

"I don't give a fuck 'bout you killing nobody. I'm hurt that you would question our daughter. I've been so good to you, better to you than your mama or Esha. I would give my life for you and the kids and all I get is questioned 'bout an ex. You don't see how your mama come in our home and start shit then hide her hands. We're at each other throat and now where is she? Any real woman would be gone right now but 'cause I love you I'm fighting through all the hell your mama has caused me. You let her do this shit, Bash. She runs you and your house when she's there and I can't take it anymore."

"Baby, I'm done. She promised to never bother us again. It's just going to be us and the kids on the other side of town. We're starting over. Now go get Kai and come home."

"Where the hell is E'shon?" I asked Bash.

"I dropped him off with his mama since I was unsure how you were going to act. I fucked up and I realized it after I said it. Once you went to laughing it only made me feel worse."

"So why did you ignore her knowing she wanted you?"

"Only to piss you off but I wasn't expecting your ass to blow up and start calling me names and shit. You feel like I'm a mama's boy?"

"I meant everything I said at the moment. The longer you with me you'll realize pissing me off is something you don't want to do."

"Can you go get my daughter and come home?"

"When is E'shon coming back?"

"She's only keeping him for one day. She can't handle herself, she damn sure ain't gon' be able to handle him. She did want me to tell you thank you for stepping in and being that mother figure for him."

"Fuck her! She over there with Kesh probably talking 'bout me like a dog."

"Actually Kesh having a hard time with the loss of Pharaoh."

I forgot about her feelings. She knew him longer than me so I know she was having a hard time. Now I wanted to reach out and make sure Cissy was okay. She loves her daddy and this was going to haunt her because it was done on national television.

"I'm sorry to hear that."

"Go ahead and get Kai and I'll be home waiting on y'all."

"Please lock my apartment back up."

"I got you, damn."

Back downstairs, the doorman was being escorted out by his boss. I was glad because it saved me the hassle of trying to prove myself against him. I later called back up there to find out why he was fired, only to find out that he had been caught having sex on the job with visitors. Karma was a nasty bitch.

20

B ash

YAHRIA SLEPT PEACEFULLY beside me while I held Kai in my arms. She was wide awake biting on her fist and staring at me like she had something to say. I don't know how I could ever question something so beautiful. It was like looking at myself when I looked at her. My mama really had my head fucked up to think I would let that dumb shit come out of my mouth was beyond me. Kai had been up for the last hour with me and I was patiently waiting for her to go to sleep. It was close to midnight and her sleep pattern was off for some reason. I told Yahria it was because she took her off the breast but she refuses to put her back on.

About a quarter to one, I eased Kai up under her mama and got out of bed. If Yahria was tired, she slept hard much like tonight. Turning the bathroom light on and closing the door, I pissed and washed my hands so I could slip in some clothes. My reflection staring back at me was a man that was willing to do what he had to do to protect his family. I knew a lot but held it in until this very moment. Yahria thought I was stupid and so did my mama but one thing about me they both didn't know, the blood that pumped through my veins was that of a street nigga. I never liked to consider myself that but I couldn't hide the fact that it was in me.

My back was against the wall and the last straw had been pulled. I slipped on my clothes and was out the door without Yahria even moving. For months now, I've known about the shit my mama was doing with Pharaoh; that's why I couldn't feel bad about what happened to him. He was like Judas to me. He traded on Yahria for a few coins and some pussy. He gets no respect from me when I know for a fact she held him down through everything. I also found out what really happened with Esha. Now, had I known that, maybe we would still be together but when I think deeper, I was glad it happened so I could meet Yahria.

Esha told me a few things that my mama did that made my stomach turn in knots. My mama was great at what she did. The woman that raised me would never hurt anyone but this new woman had no stopping point. She bluntly told me she killed the man that raised me so I knew she was capable of anything. To think that she sent Yahria through so much hell in our relationship just made me want to give her more.

My mama's car wasn't at her place but I got out anyway to see if the door was unlocked or a window. She stayed in a decent neighborhood and all the neighbors knew who I was so if someone saw me they wouldn't be suspicious. The front door was locked so I went around back because she almost always had the bathroom window up. It was down too so I was out of options here.

"She moved out. She didn't tell you?" One of the neighbors stated.

"No she didn't tell me. That's very strange. Thanks for telling me."

"Yea, the police came by today, too, and I told them the same thing. I don't know what she got herself into but you need to find out."

"Thank you sir."

She was trying to pull another fast one. That's why she kept telling me I wouldn't have to worry about her again. It was after two in the morning when I pulled back up to my condo. I was hoping she left and would never come back to cause hell for anybody else. The damage she had done would take some people a while to get over.

"Where you been?" Yahria asked.

"I went out to handle some business but I'm back now."

She didn't argue or anything; she just went back to sleep. I took all my clothes off and climbed in bed behind her since Kai was on the other side of her. Wrapping my arm around Yahria, I pulled them both in closer to me so I could feel them. My body was sleepy but my mind was racing. Yahria could tell I was tense so she flipped over and rubbed my head. She was the only one that knew that was my relaxation spot. My body started to relax and I was off to sleep.

"Wakey, wakey."

The sound of my mama voice and the cock of a gun woke me and Yahria up. I was just dreaming that my mama popped her ass up out of nowhere just to kill Yahria. Instead of waking my ass up, I continued to lay there and sleep. She stood at the foot of my bed with the gun trained on Yahria. Since having kids I didn't like to leave my guns laying around but tonight was different. I had that bitch waiting on her with one in the chamber. I picked my gun up and aimed it at her.

"Son, I just knew you were weak. You'll kill the woman that brought you in this world for a bitch that ain't got shit?"

"Bitch, I got plenty of shit. Probably more than you," Yahria told her.

"You better bring that damn voice down before I kill you sooner than expected."

"Mama, what the hell has gotten into you? You hate her that much that you willing to kill her in front of our daughter? What did she do to you?"

"She took you away from me. You are all I've ever wanted, son don't you see that? It's always been us and then you brought that crackhead bitch around and I had to get rid of her. Then you bring this thirsty bitch around."

"Mama, she didn't take me away from you. I'm still here, I'm still your son. All of us can get along just fine. Put the gun down mama before you hurt both of them," I begged.

"Son, do you know that I killed your father because I fucked up. I cheated and had you but I kept cheating because your father couldn't satisfy me like your real father could. He was a good man and he taught you how to be good man but somewhere you lost it."

"No I didn't get lost, I just started living my life."

"It doesn't matter now Subashtian."

I got up out the bed and tried to walk over to my mama. She birthed me, she would always have a spot in my heart but if she brought harm to my girl or my daughter she would no longer have a place in my life. I could see Yahria shifting in the bed to cover Kai up with her body. Yahria was tough but when a loaded gun is pointed at you, it humbles you.

"Ma, give me the gun. Yahria won't do anything to you if that's what you're afraid of."

"Subashtian, don't touch me." She tried to push me away.

Yahria took the opportunity to lunge at her but it was too late; my mama's reaction was quicker. She let off two shots in Yahria's body slumping her instantly.

"Yah...Yahria! Baby, get up!" I grabbed her body and tried to get her up. "What the fuck did you do?"

I raised my gun at my mama as my daughter screamed in the background. I couldn't hear shit and I couldn't see because of the tears stinging my eyes.

"Son, don't do this. I fixed our problem. She's gone now. It can be just me, you and E'shon," my mama pleaded.

"I don't want it that way." This was the hardest shit I had ever done but I pulled the trigger.

The End...

Please turn page!!

EPILOGUE: BASH

That night my life changed and I do mean changed. I slipped back into a deep depression after seeing Yahria laying there in her own blood. I couldn't even comfort my daughter because I just wanted her mama to come back. I couldn't do this thing called life without her. We made each other better. Yahria was my life and yes, we argued about stupid shit and yes, we curse each other but that was our love and fuck how anybody felt about our love. We made that shit work for us.

The night everything happened it was like I had to make a decision. My mama or my girl, the mother to my children. Pulling the trigger that night felt like weight being lifted off my shoulders. I pulled that trigger for Yahria, my father, Pharaoh and all the innocent people she had buried out in that wooded area. I knew her time was coming but what I didn't know was I was going to be her grim reaper.

As a man, you have to make some hard decisions but whatever you choose, make sure it's right. Have all your facts together so when that time comes, the right person gets the bullet. In my case, I believe I made the right choice. My children needed their mama more than they needed their grandma. As I cried over Yahria's body, praying that she didn't die on me, my neighbors came over and got Kai for me and made sure the police were called.

My uncle was the first detective on the scene. Instead of me going to the hospital with Yahria, I was handcuffed and placed in the back of the police car where they hauled me off and booked me for murder without even asking questions. It was me auntie Dawn that raised hell until they released me almost thirty days later. Now I knew why. My uncle was still in love with my mama. That sorry muthafucka was my daddy and he wanted me to rot in the jail because I killed the love of his life. His pussy ass made sure to stay away from me once I was released. My auntie Dawn made sure she found a loophole to get him fired and she filed for divorce.

My mama caused so much hurt and pain to so many people. I reached out to Pharaoh's family so I could help pay for the funeral. I know how the street life went which is why I got out. All we ever saw was money but never thought about death and how we didn't put the money aside for burial. I linked up with his best friend Gip and we put him away nicely. That was the least I could do. Yahria would have wanted it that way. She was hood with a heart of gold and that's what made me love her.

Another person I reached out to was Kesh. I know y'all think I'm crazy but being a single parent ain't the easiest damn thing to do. She's raising two girls without their father so I put them both some money aside to do whatever they wish when they turned eighteen. Kesh told me how much Cissy looked up to Yahria and how she loved fashion so I'm sure I knew where her money was going. Kesh was working two jobs to make sure her girls had what they needed. I tipped my hat to her for the change she had made.

As far as my life goes, I was getting better. It's never easy for you to kill your mama but she died to me that day at the table when she told me she killed my father. I lied to her when I told her I didn't watch those tapes from my old house. I sat for hours watching her do shit to Yahria, even bringing that nigga in my house while I slept. My motive was to bring her close so I could keep an eye on her but I had no idea she had just killed that girl and framed Pharaoh for it, but Yahria did. My mama was also the one that put the hit out for me to get robbed and was responsible for breaking in Yahria's apartment twice. Karma served my mama what was due to her and unfortunately it was death.

"Come on, E'shon," I called out to him as I placed the beautiful flowers on the headstone.

Kai stood by me holding my hand tightly as we waited for E'shon to run back over to us. He was still too young to understand what was going on so every time I brought him out here, he played in the dirt right next to his mama. Esha's relationship with Kesh only lasted a few months before she hooked up with a dude and ended up back on drugs. This time she didn't make it out. She overdosed and was found dead in an alley. I hated that shit had a hold of her like that but life goes on.

Kai reached for Yahria as we approached the car but I wouldn't let her pick her up because she was pregnant and didn't have no business picking Kai big behind up. Kai was spoiled rotten thanks to her mama and E'shon was your average little boy, always in some shit. Yahria's life was spared thanks to the doctors and nurses that worked tirelessly during her surgery. She took two bullets that night. One to the chest and the other to her stomach which is how we found out about her pregnancy. The bullet in her chest missed her artery by three inches but the impact of the bullet is what sent her into shock. Our daughter wasn't harmed in her stomach and was due within the next week.

"Why won't you let me pick my baby up?"

"'Cause your ass can barely walk on those swollen ankles, that's why I told you to stay home."

"I swear you kill me with that shit. I'm not sitting in the house all damn day while y'all out having fun and shit."

"Get your ass in the car, Yahria. Damn, you always want to fuss 'bout something. As long as I'm 'round and you pregnant you're not picking up shit but some food."

Yahria waved me off before getting in the car. Even with her attitude while she was pregnant, I wouldn't change anything about her. From her fuzzy hair, to her big ass ankles; I loved everything about her and couldn't wait until the day she was able to walk down the aisle. We agreed to wait until she had the baby before we got married because she wanted to get her body together and yes she was still rubbing that cocoa stuff on her stomach so she wouldn't get stretch marks. Yahria did a lot of extra shit but so what. She could do whatever she wanted as long as it was with me and the kids.

I stopped to grab us a bite to eat because she was craving hamburgers. When you got a woman that's pregnant men, just do what they ask you to do. I hated when she ate unhealthy but I was not about to get my head chewed off right now.

"You want to go in the inside or drive-thru?" I asked.

"We can go in and eat."

I let her get out while I got the kids out of their car seats. Grabbing both of their hands, I made my way into the restaurant where Yahria was waiting.

"Well, if it ain't Bash. How long has it been?"

Keysa had no idea Yahria was standing in line watching us the whole time. Shit, I was nervous because I've seen Yahria whoop my mama ass while she was pregnant.

"You can't speak 'cause you got your kids?" Keysa asked.

"Nah, bitch he can't speak 'cause he know not to speak to your hoe ass," Yahria sassed.

"Baby, let's just go somewhere else," I tried to diffuse the situation.

Yahria took heed to my word and walked out of the restaurant. I strapped the kids back in and got in the driver's seat.

"You think 'cause I'm pregnant that I won't beat that bitch ass don't you? You been fucking with her, Bash?"

"What? Hell nah!"

"You better not let me find out. With her fake ass. Ooo, I should go back in and whoop her ass for trying me."

"Baby, she didn't say anything to you," I laughed.

"Shut your damn mouth 'cause ain't shit funny."

And there you have it. This is our shit and this how we like it. Fuck all that ordinary love shit that y'all do. We fuss and we make up but we never go to bed mad at each other. Judge us all you want but I bet can't nothing penetrate what we got.

AUTHOR'S NOTES

Thank y'all so much for the love y'all been giving me for this series. I usually try to end things with two parts but stuff was so crazy in part two that I had to push out a part three. I hope that it was everything you thought it was going to be. Please don't get upset if things didn't end the way you wanted them to. We have to understand that love is different for everybody. Some of us may like a rough dudes and some of us may want that soft love. For Yahria and Bash, it ended up being both. He could love her softly and rough. Don't hate on their weirdness.

Again, thank you to all the readers for the love and support. It's greatly appreciated. Make sure you join my reading group and add me on my social media platforms to keep up with me.

Facebook: Jenica Johnson

Author page: Author Jenica Johnson

Reading Group: Jenica Johnson The Storyteller

SUBSCRIBE

Text Shan to 22828 to stay up to date with new releases, sneak peeks, contest, and more...

WANT TO BE A PART OF SHAN PRESENTS?

To submit your manuscript to Shan Presents, please send the first three chapters and synopsis to submissions@shanpresents.com

CPSIA information can be obtained
at www.ICGtesting.com
Printed in the USA
LVHW05s0035170818
587184LV00011B/960/P